"I'm so... ...uldn't have be... ...should've been as..."

Her gaze ... ...nched by the mistrust he spotted in her eyes. What kind of man did she think he was? One that held little regard for women? Oh Lord, he'd made a mess of things.

"If you truly mean that," she said, "then I'd like to be your friend, Tag."

Friend. Yes, he definitely needed friends in this new life he was making for himself here in Arizona. But did he need a friend like Emily-Ann? She made his stomach flutter and his mind turn to dreams he'd given up long ago. If he wasn't careful, she could play havoc with his peace of mind.

But for the past ten years he'd managed to keep his heart tucked safely behind an impenetrable wall. There was no reason for him to think Emily-Ann could ever breach it.

"I do truly mean it," he told her, then smiled and reached for her hand. "Let me walk you to the patio, my new friend."

She smiled back at him and as they strolled side by side through the shadows, she didn't pull her hand away from his. And Taggart couldn't summon the inner strength to let go of her.

* * *

MEN OF THE WEST: Whether ranchers or lawmen, these heartbreakers can ride, shoot— and drive a woman crazy!

Dear Reader,

Welcome back to Yavapai County, Arizona! Spring has arrived and Three Rivers Ranch is hopping with activity. Calves and foals are being born every day, hay meadows are growing, cowboys are moving the herds to greener pastures and the Hollisters are welcoming a new foreman to keep everything in order.

Widower Taggart O'Brien has arrived on Three Rivers with only one thing in mind—doing his job and doing it well. He certainly isn't looking for love. That is, until he meets Emily-Ann Broadmoor, the one and only waitress at Conchita's coffee shop. The talkative redhead is unlike any woman he's known and though he tries to squash his attraction for her, he soon finds himself yearning for coffee and pastries.

In spite of catching Camille Hollister's bridal bouquet at her friend's Christmas wedding, Emily-Ann seriously doubts she'll ever find a man to marry. Men didn't fall in love with her—they simply wanted a fun date before they moved on. She thinks Taggart is no different from the other guys who'd let her down. Yet the more time she spends with the man, the more her heart wants to believe the bridal bouquet might actually bring her true love.

I hope you enjoy reading Taggart and Emily-Ann's love story as much as I enjoyed writing it!

God bless the trails you ride,

Stella Bagwell

The Texan Tries Again

Stella Bagwell

HARLEQUIN
SPECIAL
EDITION

HARLEQUIN®
SPECIAL EDITION™

Recycling programs
for this product may
not exist in your area.

ISBN-13: 978-1-335-89447-2

The Texan Tries Again

Copyright © 2020 by Stella Bagwell

Harlequin Enterprises ULC
22 Adelaide St. West, 40th Floor
Toronto, Ontario M5H 4E3, Canada
www.Harlequin.com

Printed in U.S.A.

After writing more than eighty books for Harlequin, **Stella Bagwell** still finds it exciting to create new stories and bring her characters to life. She loves all things Western and has been married to her own real cowboy for forty-four years. Living on the south Texas coast, she also enjoys being outdoors and helping her husband care for the horses, cats and dog that call their small ranch home. The couple has one son, who teaches high school mathematics and is also an athletic director. Stella loves hearing from readers. They can contact her at stellabagwell@gmail.com.

Books by Stella Bagwell

Harlequin Special Edition

Men of the West

Her Kind of Doctor
The Arizona Lawman
Her Man on Three Rivers Ranch
A Ranger for Christmas
His Texas Runaway
Home to Blue Stallion Ranch
The Rancher's Best Gift

The Fortunes of Texas: Rambling Rose

Fortune's Texas Surprise

The Fortunes of Texas: The Lost Fortunes

Guarding His Fortune

Montana Mavericks: The Lonelyhearts Ranch

The Little Maverick Matchmaker

Visit the Author Profile page
at Harlequin.com for more titles.

To my beloved editor, Gail Chasan.
This one is for you!

Chapter One

"If I hear anyone mention that damned bridal bouquet one more time I'm going to scream," Emily-Ann Broadmoor muttered. "Catching the flowers at *your* wedding is not going to get *me* a husband. The whole idea is a silly old wives' tale. So why do you keep harping on the subject?"

Unaffected by her friend's annoyed outburst, Camille Waggoner chuckled and used her toe to push the wooden glider into a rocking motion.

From their comfortable seat beneath a large, old cottonwood, Emily-Ann could see a portion of the Hollister family, along with many friends and ranch hands, beginning to gather beneath the roof that covered the wide patio behind the Three Rivers Ranch house. Tonight, Maureen Hollister, the matriarch of the family, was throwing a barbecue for two reasons. For the first time in more than two years, Camille, the prodigal daughter, was back for a short visit. And second, the massive ranch was welcoming a new foreman.

"I'm not harping," Camille said, "and you don't think the folklore is nonsense. That's why you're afraid. That's why you don't want me, or anyone else, suggesting that your time as a single woman is coming to an end."

Emily-Ann stared at her best friend since elementary school, until the absurdity of Camille's prediction caused her to burst out laughing.

"Camille, pregnancy has done something to your brain. You're losing touch with reality."

Smiling smugly, Camille pressed her left hand to her growing belly and Emily-Ann didn't miss the diamond wedding ring sparkling on her finger. Camille Hollister had become Matthew Waggoner's wife nearly four months ago in a beautiful little Christmas ceremony down on Red Bluff, the Hollisters' second Arizona ranch.

Since then, Emily-Ann had never seen her friend so happy. And why not? After being the foreman at Three Rivers Ranch for many years, Matthew was now manager of Red Bluff, along with being one of the sexiest men to ever step foot in Yavapai County and beyond. Plus, he was madly in love with Camille. How could any woman be so lucky?

Certainly not herself, Emily-Ann thought drearily. She considered herself fortunate if she got a wink from the old man behind the meat counter at Wendell's Groceries.

"My thinking has never been clearer," Camille spoke concisely, then reached over and gave Emily-Ann's hand an affectionate pat. "I'm so glad you could make the party tonight. The two of us haven't had a chance to spend time together. Not since my wedding and that was such a hectic occasion with so many people around us that we hardly had a chance to talk."

"We've talked on the phone several times since your wedding."

Camille frowned. "Not the same. When we have a conversation I want to see you."

"You should've told me," Emily-Ann said dryly. "The next time I call we'll do FaceTime."

Camille chuckled. "That's not the same, either. So what have you been doing with yourself since the wedding? Other than running Conchita's?"

Conchita's was a little coffee and pastry shop located on a quiet street in Wickenburg. Since Emily-Ann was the only employee, other than the owner who prepared the pastries, the job kept her very busy six days a week. The salary she made was never going to do more than pay her rent and other living expenses, but she loved the job.

"I don't have time to do much," Emily-Ann reasoned.

"You're still doing online college classes, aren't you?"

Emily-Ann shrugged. "Yes. Just a few more hours and I'll get my degree. But sometimes I wonder why I chose such a field to get into. I'll probably make a miserable nurse. Taking care of a sick cat isn't like tending an ailing human."

"I happen to think you'll make a wonderful nurse. When your mother's health started to fail, you were always so good with her."

"I had to do what I could. We couldn't afford a real nurse to take care of Mom," Emily-Ann replied, not wanting to think about that especially hard time in her life.

"Well, there's always a demand for nurses." Camille smiled encouragingly. "You should be able to get a job right in Wickenburg."

"Making coffee for my friends would be far less stressful," Emily-Ann said frankly. "But Mom had a dream for me and I don't want to disappoint her."

Camille slanted her a meaningful glance. "Just like I didn't want to disappoint Dad about getting a college degree. Now your mom and my dad are both gone. But let's not dwell on that sad stuff tonight. It's party time." With a cheerful smile, Camille reached over and hooked her arm through Emily-Ann's. "And it looks like Jazelle has just arrived with a cart to restock the bar. Let's go get something to drink."

The two women walked across the backyard to join the group of people mingling on the patio. There were far more guests than Emily-Ann had expected and she was glad she'd taken extra care with her appearance this evening. Even though her mustard-colored blouse and dark green skirt weren't anything fancy they flattered her curvy figure and she'd taken the time to braid a top portion of her hair and pin it to one side. She'd never be beautiful like Camille or her sister, Vivian, but for tonight she felt as though she looked decent.

"Emily-Ann! I didn't know you had arrived!"

At the sound of the female voice, Emily-Ann turned to see Maureen Hollister hurrying toward her. The lovely woman in her midsixties gathered her up in a tight hug.

"I'm so glad you could come tonight and be with Camille," she said happily. "My two little gingers. It's just like old times seeing you girls together."

"Except that now we don't have our matching bangs and Groovy Girls dolls," Emily-Ann joked.

Maureen laughed. "Too bad you grew out of those days. But I have the dolls packed away in a trunk of toys. Someday you two might want to give them to your daughters."

"Uh—in about three months or so, if Camille has

a girl, she'll need hers," Emily-Ann told her. "But you might as well keep mine packed away in mothballs."

Maureen wagged a finger at her. "You're forgetting, honey. You caught Camille's wedding bouquet. Your time is coming!"

Laughing, Camille rolled her eyes toward Emily-Ann. "Don't scream."

Confused by her daughter's remark, Maureen frowned. "Scream? Why would she want to do something like that?"

"Nothing important," Emily-Ann answered, then quickly steered the conversation in a different direction. "Thank you for inviting me tonight, Maureen. I can't wait to eat some of Reeva's barbecue. Is there anything I can do to help in the kitchen?"

"Not a thing. I want you and Camille to stay out of the kitchen. Katherine and Vivian are helping with the food and Isabelle and Roslyn, bless their hearts, have volunteered to keep all the little ones upstairs and occupied. So everything is under control, I think." She looked at Camille. "I need to get back to the kitchen. Be sure and introduce Emily-Ann to the folks she hasn't met."

Maureen hurried away just as a group of men sauntered over to the bar, where Jazelle, the Hollisters' housekeeper, was mixing drinks. Spotting them, Camille grabbed Emily-Ann's arm and tugged her in the direction of the men.

"Come on, I want you to say hi to my brothers."

Emily-Ann had never been a bashful person and she loved meeting people, which was the main reason she loved her job at the coffee shop. But for some reason tonight, she felt hesitant about joining the group of men to say hello.

"I honestly don't think they want to waste their time with me, Camille," Emily-Ann suggested. "Let's just get a drink and go back to the glider."

Camille frowned at her. "Since when have you turned into a wallflower? Now quit being ridiculous and come on."

Camille tugged her forward and Emily-Ann had no choice but to follow her friend over to the group of men, all of whom were dressed casually in jeans and boots and various shades and styles of cowboy hats.

"Hi, guys," Camille greeted. "I thought you all might want to say hello to Emily-Ann."

Holt, the middle sibling of the Hollister clan, stepped forward with a wide grin. "I want to do more than say hi. I want a hug from Little Red."

Laughing at the nickname Holt had given her years ago, Emily-Ann hugged the tall, good-looking cowboy, who'd often been considered the wild playboy of the bunch. Now the horseman was settled down with a wife and new baby son.

"Hello, Holt." Stepping back from his affectionate hug, she smiled at him. "How does it feel to be a new father?"

The twinkle in his eyes was the same sort of joy Emily-Ann saw on Camille's face. Yes, the Hollister siblings were all happily married with children and babies now. The reality left Emily-Ann feeling as though she was standing on the porch in the cold rain, while everyone inside the house was cheery and warm and together.

"Having a son is just incredible," Holt responded to her question. "Even if I have to get up in the night to change diapers."

"Hah!" Blake, the eldest of the Hollister brothers and manager of Three Rivers Ranch, reacted with a short laugh. "I think I'll ask Isabelle just how many diapers you've changed in the wee hours of the morning."

"Not nearly as many as me," Chandler, the veterinarian of the group, boasted.

Chuckling, Joseph, the deputy and youngest Hollister, gouged an elbow in Chandler's ribs. "That's what you think, brother. Blake has us all beat. He has twins."

"Thank you, Joe," Blake said with an appreciative grin.

Camille pulled a playful face at her brothers. "I didn't bring Emily-Ann over here to listen to you four boast about your diaper changing. You're supposed to be saying hello to her."

"Hello, Emily-Ann!" they all said in loud unison.

Emily-Ann could feel a blush stinging her cheeks.

It was true she'd known the wealthy Hollister family for years, but since Camille had moved away, she'd not been here to the ranch for any reason and she felt a little awkward about showing up tonight. In spite of Camille being a dear friend, that didn't put Emily-Ann on their social calendar.

Just as that self-deprecating thought went through her mind, Blake stepped forward and gathered her up in a hug. "I see you at Conchita's fairly often, but it's nice to have you here on the ranch. Jazelle is mixing drinks. Tell me what you'd like and I'll get it."

"Not yet," Camille told him, her gaze searching the ever-growing crowd. "I thought Matthew and Tag might be over here with you guys. Where—oh, I see them coming now."

Grabbing her by the upper arm, Camille tugged her forward and Emily-Ann followed, albeit reluctantly. She was fairly acquainted with Matthew, Camille's husband, but the tall cowboy with him was a total stranger to her. A wide-brimmed cowboy hat, the color of dark coffee, shaded a tanned face with roughly honed features. His eyes were hooded beneath a pair of dark brows, while his chin jutted forward just enough to give him a dash of arrogance. Or it could be the way he was looking at her, as though she was a geek, or worse, that made him seem arrogant. Either way, Emily-Ann would've been happy to avoid the man entirely. But she couldn't escape the tight hold Camille had on her arm. Not without making a scene.

"So you two finally made it to the party?" Camille teased, directing the question mostly to her husband.

Matthew's grin was a bit guilty. "Sorry, honey, I've been showing Tag some of the more important things down at the ranch yard."

"Uh-huh," she said with a perceptive smile, "like the saddles and tack and training arena and cow barn and—"

Matthew stopped her with a laugh. "We didn't get that far," he said, then inclined his head toward Emily-Ann. "Nice to see you again, Emily-Ann. Glad you could make it to the party."

"Thank you, Matthew," Emily-Ann replied, while trying not to pay extra notice to the tall, hard-looking cowboy standing next to him. From this distance, she could see his eyes were warm brown and his hair a mixture of rust and chocolate. "It's wonderful having you and Camille back at Three Rivers. Even if it's just for a short while."

She felt Camille's hand urging her to take a step toward the foreman, and though she wanted to glower at her friend, Emily-Ann purposely kept a smile fixed upon her face.

"Tag, I'd like for you to meet Emily-Ann Broadmoor, my best friend since childhood," Camille introduced. "And Emily-Ann, this is Taggart O'Brien. He's going to be Three Rivers's new foreman."

The man's lips curved into a semblance of a polite smile and Emily-Ann found her gaze transfixed on his mouth. The lower lip was full and plush, while the top was thin and tilted upward just enough to show a glimpse of white teeth.

Extending his hand to her, he said, "Hello, Ms. Broadmoor. It's a pleasure to meet you."

A strange roaring in her ears very nearly drowned out the sound of his voice and, in spite of feeling as though she'd suddenly fallen into some sort of trance, she managed to place her hand in his.

"Thank you," she told him, while her swirling senses recognized the hard-calloused skin of his palm and the warmth of his fingers curling around hers. "Nice meeting you, too, Mr. O'Brien."

With an impatient roll of her eyes, Camille interjected, "Oh, this just won't do at all. Surely you two can use your first names. We're all family around here."

"I'm fine with it," Taggart said. "If Ms. Broadmoor doesn't mind."

"First of all, Emily-Ann is a Miss, not a Ms.," Camille corrected him, then turned a clever smile on Emily-Ann. "And she doesn't mind. Do you?"

For the life of her, she couldn't figure out why Camille was making such a big to-do out of this introduction. It wasn't like she'd be seeing the man after tonight. And from the stoic look on his face, he was totally bored by this whole meeting anyway.

Well, that was okay with her, Emily-Ann decided. She wasn't exactly thrilled about exchanging hellos with this hard-looking cowboy, either. With that thought in mind, she pulled her shoulders back and tried to forget she'd always been the poor little girl who lived on the shabby side of town.

"I don't mind," she answered, then forced her gaze back to Taggart O'Brien. "Everyone calls me Emily-Ann."

The faint smile on his lips twisted to a wider slant. "Well, everyone calls me Tag, or a few other things I shouldn't repeat."

He released her hand and Emily-Ann resisted the urge to wipe her sizzling palm against the side of her skirt.

"Tag is from West Texas," Matthew informed her. "This is his first trip to Arizona and definitely his last. The Hollisters will see to that. He's going to be a permanent fixture around here."

"Welcome to Arizona, Tag," Emily-Ann said with genuine sincerity. "I hope you like it here—in spite of the heat."

His brown eyes were roaming her face as though she had two noses or something equally strange. The sensation was definitely unsettling, she thought, almost as much as the unadorned ring finger on his left hand. Surely this sexy-looking rancher was married. From the looks of him he had to be somewhere in his thirties. Plenty old enough to have a wife and kids stashed away somewhere.

He said, "I'm used to hot weather. And from everything I've seen since I arrived, I think I'm going to like it here just fine. The Hollisters are great and the area is beautiful."

"Yes, the Hollisters are the best," Emily-Ann murmured, then purposely turned her gaze on Camille. "Uh—don't you think it's time we go get that drink?"

"Sure! I can't have anything alcoholic, but Jazelle will mix up something tasty for me." She looped her arm through Emily-Ann's, then cast a pointed look at her husband. "Would you men care to join us? It shouldn't be long before they start bringing out the food."

Smiling just for her, Matthew wrapped his hand around his wife's free arm. "I don't know about Tag, but I'd love to."

Taggart hated parties, even when they were being held partly in his honor, such as this one. He'd never been good at mixing and mingling with people and being single made everything more awkward when he was introduced to the unwed women in the group. He didn't have a wife to help him escape unwanted company, or to give him a reason to excuse himself.

Yet in this case, he wasn't looking around for an escape route. Emily-Ann Broadmoor didn't appear to be one of those boring cookie-cutter young women who spent hours trying to improve their appearance and five minutes or less educating themselves on things that actually mattered.

She wasn't batting her long lashes at him or slanting him a coy look. She wasn't grabbing his arm and hanging on as though she'd suddenly lost the strength to stand on her own two feet. No, this woman was refreshingly different, he thought. She might even be one he'd like to get to know as a friend. There couldn't be any harm in that, he assured himself.

"I'm more than ready for a drink and dinner." Purposely stepping up to the pretty redhead's side, he offered her his arm. "What about you, Emily-Ann?"

For a moment he thought she was going to ignore him or simply walk away, but then she smiled and wrapped an arm through his.

"Thank you, Tag."

The four of them moved slowly through the crowd toward the bar area where the four Hollister brothers were sipping cocktails and chatting with a few of the ranch hands. It was a sight that Taggart would've never seen on the Flying W back in Texas. Once the Armstrong family had taken over, the hands were never invited to mix with the employers, unless it was to take orders.

Hoping to shake away the unpleasant thoughts, he glanced down at Emily-Ann. She wasn't exactly a beautiful woman, but she was very pretty in a unique sort of way. Her square face had a wide plush mouth, high cheekbones and a sprinkling of pale freckles across the bridge of her upturned nose. Long brown lashes shaded eyes that were emerald green. Or, at least, that had been his first impression of their color. Until she'd turned her head and the light had hit them from a different angle. Then her eyes had taken on the color of a spring leaf that hadn't yet ripened in the sun.

"Do you come out here to the ranch often?" he asked her as they followed Matthew and Camille through a group of milling guests.

"When Camille lived here I visited the ranch quite often. Now I don't have much reason to drive out here. Most of the family stops by the coffee shop where I work, so I see them regularly."

Ahead of them, Matthew and Camille paused to acknowledge a small group of old acquaintants. While Taggart and Emily-Ann stood waiting, he turned his gaze back to the redhead. And suddenly he wished the gentleman in him had never offered his arm to this woman. The casual touch of her hand was causing hot sparks to shoot all the way up to his shoulder, making it difficult to concentrate.

Doing his damnedest to ignore the unexpected reaction, he tried to focus on her last remarks. "You work as a waitress?" he asked.

"I guess you could call me a waitress," she told him. "The coffee shop is small and I run it by myself. The owner does the pastry baking, then leaves everything else up to me."

"I'd never be able to do your job," he told her. "I'd end up eating all the profits."

The smile on her face drew him like a warm fire on a frigid night and he silently cursed himself for being so responsive to her. He was in no position to be feeling such things toward any woman.

A week had hardly passed since he'd arrived here on the ranch. Boxes of his belongings were still stacked in the modest house where Matthew had lived during his tenure as the ranch's foreman. What with getting to know the Hollister family and learning his way around the ranch, he'd hardly had a chance to draw a good breath, much less unpack. He didn't have time for a woman. And even if he did, he wasn't in the market for marriage or even a serious affair. Furthermore, he never would be.

Her rich voice suddenly broke into his dire thoughts. "Once you have one of Conchita's pastries you're hooked. I try not to eat them, but it's a fight. Now Holt's wife, Isabelle, is a different matter. She comes in and eats a pile of brownies or whatever she wants and never gains an ounce. It isn't fair. Little Carter hasn't turned a month old yet and Isabelle already looks great. Must be all that horseback riding she does."

Taggart could've told Emily-Ann, she had no cause to worry about her figure. It was nice. Hell, it was more than nice, he thought. She was curvy in all the right places and he had no doubt she'd feel soft in his arms. Just the way a woman ought to feel.

The unsettling thought forced him to clear his throat. "Do you ride horses?" he asked.

She nodded. "When Camille and I were much younger we rode all over the ranch," she answered, then went on in a pensive voice, "Because she was my friend I got the chance to do things that I couldn't have done otherwise. But now, working and taking classes doesn't leave me much leisure time. And with Camille living at Red Bluff things have changed. But then you already know that. I mean, you're here because Matthew runs Red Bluff ranch now."

"Yes, that's why I'm here. To try to fill his boots," he said wryly. "It's not going to be an easy job."

She smiled at him. "If Blake and Maureen believe you can do the job, then I'm positive you can."

He was thinking how the confidence in her voice made him feel just a bit taller when Matthew and Camille turned back to them.

"Sorry about that," Matthew said. "Everyone wants to talk. You'd think I'd been gone for five years instead of five months."

Camille slanted a loving glance at her husband. "Shows how well you're thought of around here."

The first time Taggart had met Matthew and Camille, he'd not missed the affection that naturally flowed back and forth between the newlyweds. It was obvious they were deeply in love and though he was happy for them, seeing them together was a constant reminder of all that he'd lost. All that he'd never have.

"My wife is trying her best to give me the big head," Matthew said with a chuckle, then gently nudged Camille onward.

The four of them moseyed on through the crowd until they reached the long bar constructed of native rock and topped with rough cedar boards. Behind the rustic counter, Jazelle, a young blond-haired woman was pouring a hefty amount of tequila into a tall pitcher of margarita mix.

"Oh, I'll take one of those, Jazelle," Emily-Ann spoke up.

"Same for me," Taggart added his request.

Jazelle poured the concoction over two iced glasses and handed them over, while Camille continued to study the large assortment of refreshments lined up on the counter.

"I can't make up my mind," she said after a moment.

After giving his wife an indulgent smile, Matthew said to Jazelle, "I know what I want. Just give me plain ole coffee."

Camille groaned. "That's too hot. I want something sweet and cold."

"We know Camille can't have alcohol so just give her tomato juice," Emily-Ann joked. "Or water."

Pulling a face at Emily-Ann, Camille said, "Don't listen to her, Jazelle. She doesn't know about cravings. She's never been pregnant."

"No. I haven't been pregnant," Emily-Ann replied. "And I'm beginning to think I'll never be."

"Oh, come on, Emily-Ann," Jazelle teased, "I wouldn't be saying anything like that. You caught Camille's wedding bouquet. You know what that means."

Somewhat puzzled by the whole exchange between the women, Taggart watched a dark blush steal across Emily-Ann's cheeks. The added color made her face even prettier, he decided.

"All right, that does it!" Emily-Ann muttered. "As soon as I down this margarita, I'm going home and tearing that damned bouquet into shreds and throwing it in the trash can."

Instead of getting angry at her friend's ominous threat, Camille burst out laughing. "Sorry, Emily-Ann, but you're not going anywhere—except to the dinner with your friends. Tag, just grab her arm if she tries to leave."

Taggart had no way of knowing what exactly the women were arguing about, other than it had something to do with a wedding bouquet. The word had seemed to set off a mild explosion in Emily-Ann. And why had she said that about never being pregnant? Was there a reason she couldn't have, or didn't want, children? Maybe she was one of those women who decided motherhood is not for her. But Taggart seriously doubted that. Her body moved with a sensuality that said she was made to make love to a man.

"I'm not sure I should try that," Taggart said. "She's a redhead. She might slap me."

Camille laughed again, while Emily-Ann gazed over the rim of her frosted glass at him.

"I'm sorry, Tag," she said, then smiled impishly. "I'm not really bad-tempered. Until I get around my old friend."

He was about to tell her that he wasn't thinking she was bad-tempered when Blake suddenly appeared at his side and clamped a friendly hand on his shoulder.

"Sorry to interrupt, Tag, but there's a group of men from the cattlemen's association who are anxious to meet you."

"Sure," he said, but as he walked away with the ranch manager, he wondered if he'd get a chance to talk with Emily-Ann again before the night was over. And wondered, too, why he'd want to.

Chapter Two

Damn it all, Taggart O'Brien had already ruined her evening, Emily-Ann silently cursed. She'd been looking forward to seeing the Hollisters and spending time with Camille. Now she couldn't focus on anything, except the tall Texan with warm brown eyes and slow, melting smile.

Absently pushing a pile of brisket and potato salad around her plate, she lowered her lashes and glanced at the object of her thoughts. He was sitting across the portable table and three chairs down from hers. Since everyone had sat down to eat, Matthew and the Hollister brothers had consumed Taggart's attention, but that hadn't lessened the impact of his presence.

Before the party had started this evening, Camille had told Emily-Ann how the whole family had nothing but praise for the man. At the time, Emily-Ann hadn't taken much note of her friend's chatter about the newly hired foreman. After all, she'd never be crossing paths with the man. But now that she'd stood close to him, looked into his brown eyes and felt the hard warmth of his arm beneath her hand, her thoughts were spinning with questions about him.

Her reaction to him was worse than foolhardy, Emily-Ann thought ruefully. All she had to do was glance at him to know he could have his pick of women. And for all she knew, he might have a special one tucked away somewhere. Most likely back in Texas where he'd migrated from. Yet those assumptions did little to stop the race of her pulse when she looked in his direction. Nor did they stop her from wondering if she might have the opportunity to speak with him again before the party ended and she headed home to Wickenburg.

"Are you angry with me?"

Camille's question had Emily-Ann turning a look of surprise on her friend. "Why, no," she said. "Why would you think that?"

"You've not said more than ten words since we sat down. And instead of eating, you've been using your food to build a dam across your plate."

Shaking her head, Emily-Ann said, "There's nothing wrong. I guess the margarita ruined my appetite."

Camille hardly looked convinced. "Look, I'm sorry I teased you so about the bouquet. As far as I'm concerned, you can toss it in the garbage. I won't say another word about it."

Feeling more than a little ashamed of herself, Emily-Ann smiled at her. "Don't be silly. I'm not angry at you. And I'm not about to throw the bouquet away. Why should I? It's probably the closest thing I'll ever have to bridal flowers."

"Well, if I hurt your feelings—"

Emily-Ann let out a good-natured groan. "You're being ridiculous now. You could never hurt my feelings. So tease all you want."

"So if it's not me, then what is it?" Camille persisted. "In all our years as friends I've never seen you this quiet."

Emily-Ann shrugged. "Sorry. I guess I've been thinking a lot tonight. Seeing your family and how much things have changed in the past few years. In some ways it makes me a little melancholy."

Camille reached over and squeezed Emily-Ann's hand. "But we're all so happy now," she said. "Even Mother is really smiling again."

Yes, Emily-Ann had noticed how cheerful Maureen seemed tonight. She'd also observed how Gil Hollister, brother to Maureen's late husband, Joel, was never very far from the woman's side. Emily-Ann had met the man a long time ago, during one of his brief visits to the ranch, but over the past years, she'd not seen or heard much about him. Other than the fact that he worked as a detective on the Phoenix police force. Then a few months ago, at Camille's wedding, word began to spread that after thirty years of service, the man had retired and was moving back to Yavapai County.

"I am glad about that," Emily-Ann said. "There for a while it was like the real Maureen had gone into hiding."

Camille nodded and Emily-Ann watched her friend's eyes travel down the table to where Maureen and Gil were sitting side by side. In many ways, the man in his sixties reminded Emily-Ann of Joel, Camille's late father. Although Gil's hair was graying somewhat, the dark sections that remained were the same color that Joel's had been and he also possessed the same strong, stocky build as his brother.

"I think Uncle Gil is making a big difference in her life," Camille said thoughtfully.

Emily-Ann searched her friend's face. "Are you and your brothers okay with that? I mean, I know how much you all adored your father. Maybe you're thinking your uncle is trying to move in and take his place."

Camille released a heartfelt sigh. "Daddy was ten feet tall to all of us. No one could ever replace him. But as far as I'm concerned I don't want Mother pining her life away for someone who can never come back. I can't say for sure how each of my brothers feel, but I do know they want Mother's life to be full and happy."

Several years ago, Joel's body had been discovered out on the range not far from the ranch yard. His boot was still hung in the stirrup and he'd obviously been dragged for miles before the horse he'd been riding had finally come to a halt. The family and anyone who'd ever known Joel Hollister had been devastated by his untimely death.

Emily-Ann had hurt for the loss her friend had endured. Even so, she knew that Camille had been blessed for having a father for nineteen years. Emily-Ann had never had one. Not a real father, anyway.

"Yes, I'm sure your brothers feel that way," Emily-Ann said thoughtfully. "And your uncle seems like a genuine kind of guy."

"I think so, too," Camille replied, then smiling she pointed to the food on Emily-Ann's plate. "Eat. Before you turn that stuff into a pile of hash."

It wasn't until hours later, after most of the guests had gone, that Taggart slipped away from the handful of people left on the patio and walked around to the side of the house where a view of the ranch yard could be seen in the distance.

Leaning his shoulder against the large trunk of a cottonwood tree, he gazed out at the numerous barns and sheds and endless maze of connecting corrals. Before he'd ever thought about leaving West Texas and the Flying W behind, he'd heard of Three Rivers Ranch. It had a reputation for prestigious horses and crossbred cattle that could thrive under the harshest conditions. Taggart had expected the livestock to be top-notch. What he hadn't expected was the sheer vastness of the property. Even by Texas standards it was massive and rough and beautiful.

"Did you decide you needed a little peace and quiet?"

The female voice startled him and he glanced around to see Emily-Ann stepping out of the deep shadows. He'd not known anyone was around and he wondered if she'd been watching him. The idea sent a shaft of heat slithering down his backbone.

"Something like that," he answered, then asked, "What about you?"

She joined him beneath the tree. "I've been up-stairs to see the kids and the babies. Billy, Chandler's baby, is teething now and yelling up a storm. He makes that coyote out there in the hills sound wimpy."

Taggart chuckled. "Doc will be proud to hear his new son has stronger vocal cords than a coyote."

She didn't make a reply and Taggart glanced over to see she was gazing thoughtfully out at the ranch yard. In many ways, she seemed at home here on Three Rivers, but in other ways, he sensed that she felt apart from the Hollisters and their friends. Although, he couldn't imagine why that would be. They all treated her like a family member.

Because she was my friend I got the chance to do things that I couldn't have done otherwise.

Her remark about Camille had struck Taggart and left him wondering what she'd meant by it exactly. That the Hollisters being rich made them different from her? Well, that was hardly a surprise. The Hollisters' wealth superseded most everyone in the area, including him.

"Is this place anything like the ranch where you worked before?" she asked.

Her question brought him out of his reverie and as he continued to rest his weight against the tree trunk, he allowed his gaze to linger on her face and hair. At the moment, it was splotched with moonlight and he couldn't help but wonder what it would be like to kiss the silvery spots upon her skin.

"The Flying W was big, but not this big. There weren't any mountains on it, but there were lots of what we Texans call cuts and breaks. It's where the years of rain and wind create deep gorges and cut banks into the ground."

"What about trees? Did you have many of those?"

"Some blue cedar and cottonwood. But they were few and far between and the wind usually kept most of the leaves stripped off the cottonwoods. That's the way it is up near the panhandle. But there was plenty of cholla cactus and it's real pretty when it blooms."

"Sounds desolate," she commented.

"I suppose it is—in a way. But it was home to me."

He could feel those green eyes of hers studying his face and though they were partially covered by shadows, he knew they were full of questions. Many of which he didn't feel comfortable answering. Not now. Maybe after this place began to feel like home to him, he'd want to talk about his life back in Texas.

He said, "Now you're thinking if I felt that way, why did I ever leave. Right?"

"It did cross my mind," she admitted. "But you don't have to tell me. That's your business. Not mine."

She was exactly right. And he should feel glad that she respected his privacy. Yet a part of him was disappointed that she wasn't interested enough to pry at him. Had moving to Arizona turned him into a wishy-washy fool, he suddenly wondered? Or was this sexy redhead the reason his thought process had gone haywire?

"The Williamsons, the people who owned the Flying W, were great to work for. I started as a day hand there when I was twenty-two. Three years later I'd worked my way up to foreman."

"Sounds like Matthew. He was very young when he first started working here on Three Rivers."

"Matthew has been blessed and he knows it. The Hollisters will always be here. They'll always hold the reins. He's never had to worry that a syndicate or some other owner would come in and start changing the way the ranch should be run."

"And that's what happened at the Flying W?" she asked.

Nodding, he tried not to feel bitter. His old job was behind him now and the problems there would continue to go on without him.

"The Williamsons built the ranch years ago and owned it, up until a year ago," he explained. "But then Mr. Williamson, who's in his mideighties, suffered a mild stroke. He recovered nicely, but his daughter didn't waste time in persuading him to sell the property. She convinced him that the ranch was the reason for his stroke."

"Was it?" Emily-Ann asked.

The choked sound he made was intended to be a laugh, but it held no humor. "That was a joke. She was the reason the old man carried around a load of stress. She'd been married and divorced twice and the cost of her mistakes had pretty much bankrupted her parents. So he sold to a family from Georgia. The Armstrongs know nothing about the West or raising cattle. Nor do they want to learn. So you can pretty much figure out the problems that caused for me and all the hands."

"Were you the only one who left the ranch's employment? Or did the other hands feel like you and leave, too?"

"All the original crew of men who worked the Flying W have left and gone on to different jobs now. I was one of the last holdouts. I guess I was foolishly hoping that something would change. That Mr. Williamson would find a way to buy the ranch back. But it never happened."

She looked at him. "I'm going to assume that the daughter was an only child. There were no other children to help with the ranch or the finances?"

Taggart shook his head. He'd been the closest thing to a son to Walt Williamson. But Emily-Ann didn't need to know that. Nor did she need to know that the daughter had always been bad-mouthing Taggart because he refused to warm up to her sexual propositions.

"Unfortunately, Joanna was the only child the couple had. Things might have been different if there'd been another grown son or daughter or around the ranch."

She moved a step closer and Taggart caught the gentle scent of flowers and desert wind on her hair. The fragrance was alluring and unique, just like her.

"Well, I don't know about the other men you worked with on the Flying W and whether they've moved on to better things. But you certainly have. You're going to love working for the Hollisters. They're fair and honest and they care for their cattle and horses the same way their forefathers did a hundred and fifty years ago."

The sight of her upturned face grabbed something inside of him and to save himself from doing or saying something idiotic, he forced his gaze back on the ranch yard.

"Yes. I've learned this place has a long, colorful history," he said. "I feel honored to be a part of it now."

She smiled. "I'm guessing your family probably wasn't keen on you moving away to another state."

As always when he thought of his parents, a part of him shuttered down. It had been so long since all of his family had been together and even then, his father had never really put his wife and children before himself. His mother had worked hard to put meals on the table and made sure that Taggart and his little sister were clean and cared for. She'd been the rock that had held them all together.

"My mother has been dead for a long time and my father, such as he is, only comes around when he wants something. I do have a younger sister, Tallulah. We're close."

"Does she live in Texas?"

"Yes, in a little town close to the New Mexico line." He looked back at her. "What about you? Do your parents or siblings live around here?"

She looked away from him and for a moment Taggart thought she was going to totally ignore his question and then she finally spoke in a small voice.

"My mother passed away a few years ago," she said. "And my father was—never in my life. I don't have any siblings. I wish I did. I think things would've been a lot better if I'd had a brother or sister. But it didn't turn out that way."

It was easy to tell from the strained sound of her voice that it was difficult for her to talk about her family, or lack of one. Taggart could have told her that he understood, that he, too, had come from a broken home. But he'd already told this woman much more than he should have. In fact, he couldn't believe he'd told her all those things about the Flying W or his parents. It wasn't like him to divulge such personal things about himself to anyone.

Down toward the ranch yard, he could hear a few penned calves bawling and farther on a stallion called to his mares. The familiar sounds were comforting to Taggart, but apparently Emily-Ann hadn't taken notice of them. She was focusing on the lonesome wail of a coyote far off on a ridge of mountains west of the ranch house.

"When I was a young girl I used to be afraid when I heard a coyote," she said wryly. "I was a town girl and didn't know much about the outdoors. Camille told me that coyotes are very family oriented and that when they mate it's for life. I never did really believe her. She's such a romantic I figured she made it up. Because the whole thing sounded so dreamy and tender."

He grunted while wishing a part of him could still feel loving and tender. But there were no soft spots left in his heart, no room for a romantic dream to dwell and grow.

"I can assure you that Camille told you right. Coyotes do mate for life. So do mourning doves—until one of the pair dies."

Until one dies. Yes, Taggart had mated for life, he thought. Only that life hadn't lasted long.

"Oh," she said, then laughed softly, "I've learned something tonight. Mainly that I should believe Camille when she tells me something."

He pushed away from the tree trunk. This wasn't good, he thought. Standing out here in the shadows with a voluptuous redhead that smelled like an angel and looked like a seductress.

"I should get back to the patio," he said. "Most of the guests are leaving and the Hollisters are probably wondering where I've gotten off to."

"Time I was going, too. The drive back to my house takes about thirty minutes and I have to open Conchita's early in the morning." Smiling at him, she offered him her hand. "I've enjoyed talking with you, Tag. And I wish you the best with your new job. Maybe one of these days you'll get the urge for a pastry and some coffee and drop by Conchita's. It's open every day but Sunday."

His fingers tightened around hers and before he knew what he was doing he was tugging her forward until the front of her body was very nearly touching his.

She looked up at him and Taggart's gaze took in her wide green eyes and parted lips. She was clearly surprised by his action, but not nearly as stunned as he was feeling.

"Tag, what—"

"I couldn't let you walk off," he said. "Not until I told you how much I've enjoyed these few minutes with you."

Her breasts rose and fell as she drew in a deep breath, then quickly exhaled. "If you really got to know me, you wouldn't be saying that."

Her hand felt so soft and warm that all he could think of was pulling her closer, letting his hands roam her back and his lips explore hers.

"Why?"

He watched her teeth bite into her bottom lip. "Because I'm not your kind of woman."

That was far from what he was expecting her to say. "I wonder how you came to that conclusion. You don't know me—yet."

Her nostrils flared and he could see a vein at the base of her throat throbbing at a rapid pace. It was obvious he was making her nervous, but she was doing a hell of a lot more to him than that. Just holding her hand, feeling the heat of her body radiating toward his was enough to stir a flame deep inside him.

Her lips twisted with wry resignation. "Let's just

say I know my limitations. And you're on the other side of the boundary. But it would be nice to be your friend, Tag. I'd like that."

Maybe she'd like things that way, Taggart thought, but he wouldn't. At some point from the moment he'd met her a few hours ago, until now, his mind had tossed away the idea of wanting to be her friend and changed to wanting to get to know every inch of her. The idea was shocking and scary, but it was there in his head anyway and he couldn't get it out.

"That's not the way I see things, Emily-Ann. I'm seeing you in my arms—like this."

Confusion flashed in her eyes, then she opened her mouth to speak, but he didn't wait to hear her reply. Instead, he bent his head and placed his lips over hers.

Soft, sweet and velvety smooth. Her lips were all that and more. And for a long, long moment Taggart lost himself in the pleasure of kissing her.

It wasn't until his arms slipped around her waist and he felt her hands fluttering helplessly against his chest that he realized he had to end the contact. Otherwise his senses were going to forget where he was, and why a kiss was all he dare take from this woman.

Forcing his head up, he drew in a ragged breath and watched her eyelids flutter open. He saw surprise flickering in the green depths and something else he couldn't quite identify. Was that longing, or regret, or a mixture of the two?

It doesn't matter, Tag. You can't get caught up in what this woman is thinking or feeling!

The voice in his head made him want to curse out loud. Instead, he did his best to smile and act as though her kiss hadn't shaken him all the way to the soles of his boots.

"You go around locking lips with women you've only known a few hours?" she asked.

The husky note in her voice was such a sexy sound it made him want to pull her back into his arms and kiss her all over again.

"Uh—no. I don't normally—kiss any woman." His throat felt raspy and he tried to swallow the sensation away as he lifted his hat from his head and swiped a hand through his hair. "Must be something about the moonlight."

An incredulous look appeared in her eyes and then she let out a cynical snort. "Aww, shucks ma'am, I just couldn't help myself," she said in an exaggerated drawl. "Am I going to hear that next?"

"No. And you're way off on the accent. I'm not from South Texas. I'm from West Texas."

Her nostrils flared. "There's a difference?"

"A huge one."

Something flashed in her eyes and then her gaze dropped to the middle of his chest. "Sorry. I shouldn't have been so flippant," she mumbled. "But you have the wrong idea about me."

Long brown lashes were veiling her eyes, yet he could see enough of her lips to know they were trembling. Damn it, he'd never intended to insult her.

"No. I got the wrong idea about myself," he said flatly. "I'm sorry. And you're right. I shouldn't have been kissing you. Instead, I should've been asking you to be my friend."

Her gaze lifted to his and Taggart felt punched by the mistrust he spotted in her eyes. What kind of man did she think he was? One that held little regard for women? Oh Lord, he'd made a mess of things.

"If you truly mean that," she said, "then I'd like to be your friend, Tag."

Friend. Yes, he definitely needed friends in this new life he was making for himself here in Arizona. But did he need a friend like Emily-Ann? She made his stomach flutter and his mind turn to dreams he'd given up long ago. If he wasn't careful she could play havoc with his peace of mind.

But for the past ten years he'd managed to keep his heart tucked safely behind an impenetrable wall. There was no reason for him to think Emily-Ann could ever breach it.

"I do truly mean it," he told her, then smiled and reached for her hand. "Let me walk you to the patio, my new friend."

She smiled back at him and as they strolled side by side through the shadows, she didn't pull her hand away from his. And Taggart couldn't summon the inner strength to let go of her.

Chapter Three

Human anatomy. Learning the subject was far more difficult than Emily-Ann had expected and she wondered for the umpteenth time why she'd ever believed she could acquire a nursing degree. A person needed a high intelligence and laser focus to make it through chemistry, physiology, microbiology and all the other terrifying classes that ended in y. Emily-Ann possessed neither of those attributes. Especially the focus part.

Ever since she'd gone to the Hollister party a little over a week ago, she'd been going around in a goofy daze and trying, without much success, to shake Taggart O'Brien from her mind. She still couldn't figure out why the man had taken the time to have a conversation with her, much less kiss her.

When she'd walked upon him in the darkness, she'd not intended to strike up a conversation with the man, much less get tangled up in his arms. She'd simply planned to acknowledge his presence with a few words, then move on. But that plan had quickly gone awry and now, days later, her mind was jammed with thoughts and questions about the man.

Forget the long, tall Texan, Emily-Ann. He's more than trouble. He's a walking heartache. That phony explanation of why he'd kissed you was pathetic. You know exactly what that little embrace had been about. He was just testing the waters, trying to see if you'd be willing to go to bed with him. That's all any man wants from you, sweetie. A tumble between the sheets and a goodbye kiss.

The taunting voice in her head caused her to close the textbook with a loud snap and a long sigh. She was wasting time trying to concentrate on her studies, she decided. And anyway, the clock on the wall said it was a quarter to three. It was time to start shutting the coffee shop up for the evening.

Sliding off one of the wooden chairs provided for the customers, she walked behind the tall glass display case that served as a counter and stuffed the textbook into a duffel bag she'd stored on a shelf against the wall.

Up until an hour ago, she'd seen a steady stream

of customers all day. Now there were only a few pastries left on the red plastic trays inside the display case. Conchita would definitely be pleased with the sales, she thought, as she began to load the leftovers into white paper sacks.

She was halfway through the task when the bells fastened over the door facing jingled, announcing that someone had entered the shop. It never failed, she thought, as she finished placing a baked donut covered with nuts into a sack. The minute she started to put everything away, someone wanted to come in for coffee or pastries, or both.

Glancing through the front glass of the display case, she could see the customer was a man wearing blue jeans and worn brown boots covered with dust. Other than the Hollisters, she didn't get too many cowboys in the place, especially at this time of day.

"I'm closing, but you're welcome to get a take-out order." She pulled her head from the case and raised up to find herself looking straight into Taggart O'Brien's face.

A slow smile creased his cheeks. "Hello, Emily-Ann. Looks like I picked a bad time to come in."

Anytime would be a bad time for her peace of mind, she thought. Especially when just looking at him set her heart thumping like a rocket about to shoot into space.

She nervously swiped the tip of her tongue over her lips. "No problem. I'm just dealing with the pastries that were left over from this morning. Whatever doesn't sell I drop off at the local nursing homes. The residents love getting them."

"That's a nice gesture," he said.

She shrugged one shoulder while wondering why he'd showed up today. For a day or two after the Hollister party, she'd thought, even hoped, that he'd come by to say hello. But after more than a week passed, she'd given up and decided he'd forgotten all about her.

"I like seeing the smiles on the old people's faces whenever I walk in," she told him.

"I'm smiling. I hope you're liking mine," he said in a teasing voice.

As he walked up to the glass counter, Emily-Ann's gaze traveled over his face and she realized his image was even more striking than the one she remembered at the party. Seeing him in the light of day, his complexion was a much darker brown and so was his hair. The arrogant chin was more like a concrete abutment, but that feature was definitely softened by the faint dimples bracketing his lips.

Had she actually kissed that mouth? The mere idea caused a shiver to slide down her spine.

"It's nice to see you again, Tag," she said, while hoping her voice sounded casual to his ear. "You're a long distance from Three Rivers. What brings you to town?"

"I got a hankering for pastries."

It felt like his gaze was swarming all over her and she wondered what he was thinking. That she looked rather plain in her brown shirt and faded blue jeans?

As her fingers fiddled with the long red braid lying across her shoulder, she assured herself that it didn't matter if her makeup had disappeared hours ago. She didn't want to impress this man. She wanted to forget him. Well, sort of.

"I don't know about the bunkhouse cook, but I know that Reeva, the Hollisters' cook, keeps all kinds of sweets made for the family. I'm sure she'd be happy to serve you some of them—whenever you get a hankering."

He chuckled. "Well, I did have to make a trip to the saddle shop. So I'm treating myself now. That is, if I'm not too late to get something."

Emily-Ann couldn't help it. She was so happy to see him, she couldn't act cool if she tried.

Smiling, she said, "It's not too late at all. What would you like?"

He gazed at the baked goods that were left in the display cabinet. "Hmm. I'm partial to chocolate so give me a brownie and what is that round thing that's covered in chocolate?" he asked. "It looks good, too."

"That's a Bismarck. It's like a donut covered in chocolate icing and the center is filled with custard."

"I'll take that, too. But if you've already drained the coffeepot, I'll just drink water."

"No problem. I can make a single cup for you.

Want to have a seat?" She gestured to the little square table where she'd been sitting only minutes before he'd arrived. "Or you might like to sit outside. The weather has been beautiful today."

"I'd rather eat outside—if you can join me," he said.

"I'd love to," she told him. "Like I said, I was closing up anyway."

While she gathered the pastries he wanted and made the coffee, he meandered around the small room, studying the old local memorabilia that adorned the walls, particularly photos of Wickenburg in its early, gold rush days.

"This is interesting," he said. "I like history. It makes us who we are, don't you think?"

"Yes," she agreed. "In more ways than most people imagine."

With the coffee done, she carried the cup and a small tray holding the pastries out to him.

"If you want anything in your coffee, it's all over there." She pointed to a small table containing all sorts of creamers, milk, sugar and sweeteners.

"No thanks. I like it black." He took the goodies from her, then asked, "Aren't you going to have something with me? At least some coffee. I hate to eat without you having something, too."

She groaned, while thinking the temptation of spending time with him was far stronger than the call of her sweet tooth. "Well, since I didn't eat lunch I suppose I could have a brownie," she said. "Just give me a minute and I'll make another cup of coffee."

Once she had her food and drink, the two of them walked outside to where a group of three small wrought iron tables and chairs were grouped beneath the lacy shade of two mesquite trees.

At a table nearest to the stone walkway leading up to the building, he pulled out one of the chairs and helped her into it. Once he was comfortably seated across from her, she asked, "So how has your new job been going?"

One corner of his lips curved upward. "It's been going well, I think. I've not had any complaints from Blake and Maureen yet. They have far more confidence in me than I do in myself. And they seem to understand I need time to learn the ranch—and the men."

She thoughtfully sipped her coffee. "Have the guys all accepted you as their new boss?"

"That's my biggest concern. Because if I don't have their respect I'm going to have problems. And since they all thought Matthew could walk on water that makes him a tough act to follow. But I'm trying. And so far they've all seemed fairly receptive of me. I don't know for sure, but I expect that's because Blake probably laid down the law to them before I ever arrived."

She pinched off a bite of brownie. "You're selling yourself short, Tag. The Hollisters don't have stupid men working for them. They can see you know your business."

The full-fledged smile he shot her caused her breath to momentarily hang in her throat. How could a man who looked like this still be single? It didn't seem possible.

He's single, you ninny, because he wants to be that way. He's thirty-two. He's had plenty of time to marry if he'd wanted to.

Mentally shaking herself, she sipped more coffee, while across from her, he ate the brownie in four bites then started on the Bismarck.

"Can you see that I know my business?" he asked with a soft chuckle.

Her cheeks suddenly felt hot. "Uh—well, I've not seen you in action. And I don't exactly know the things that a ranch foreman does, but you look like you'd be very comfortable on a horse—with a rope in your hand. This town is full of cowboys and after a while it's easy to tell which ones are genuine and who's trying to play the part."

Amusement crinkled the corners of his eyes. "I'm relieved to hear I look genuine."

As Emily-Ann nibbled her way through the chocolate dessert, she couldn't help but wonder if he'd thought about their kiss. Probably not the way she'd thought about it. Not the way she'd obsessed over the taste of his lips, the scent of his hair and skin, and the hardness of his body. Hopefully in a few more days the memories would dim. But for now they were as fresh as though it had just happened.

"The other night at the party, did I hear you mention that you were taking some sort of classes?"

Surprised that he'd remembered, she said, "Yes. I'm taking online classes to become an RN."

"A nurse. That's an ambitious choice. So I guess that means you don't always plan to work here at the coffee shop."

She glanced over her shoulder at the small square building with slab pine siding and a tiny covered porch, then turned her gaze back to him. "I love working here. But it pays just enough for me to get by. And my mother had a dream for me to be a nurse."

"What about your own dreams?"

She'd not expected that kind of question from him. In fact, Camille and Maureen were the only two people who'd ever asked her about her private wants and wishes.

"A minute ago you mentioned ambition, but I've never really had much of that, Tag. If it wasn't for me making a promise to my mother before she died, I doubt I'd be pushing myself to get a nursing degree. I'd probably be content to just sell coffee and donuts and keep living in the same little house that I grew up in."

"Nothing wrong with that if you're happy. Money, and the things it can buy, doesn't necessarily equal happiness. I know. I saw it firsthand with the Armstrong family. Cold and bitter. The whole bunch of them."

"Well, I don't want to become a nurse just to make a better salary. And deep down, I'm not doing it just to follow my mother's dream. I've thought about it long and hard and even though I'm not exactly ambitious, I'm drawn to the idea of helping people. You see, Mom was in bad health for a couple of years before she passed away. I saw how much it meant for her to have the right care."

"If it means anything I think you have the nature for nursing, Emily-Ann. And since you're studying to be a nurse, do you have any suggestions to treat a horse bite?"

She frowned. "You've been bitten by a horse?"

He put down his coffee cup and pushed up the sleeve of his pale blue shirt. As Emily-Ann caught a glimpse of the wounds on his forearm, she took hold of his hand and pulled it across the table toward her.

"This is serious, Tag." She studied the crescent-shaped tears that appeared to go deep into the flesh of his forearm. The gashes were an angry red with dried blood crusted around the edges. "You need a tetanus shot and possibly some stitches. How did that happen?"

"I was playing with one of Holt's young stallions and made the mistake of turning my back on him. He nabbed me on the arm to let me know he wanted the game to keep going. I'm going to stop by Doc's animal clinic on the way home. He'll take care of it."

She rolled her eyes. "We do have regular doctors here in town. No need for you to go to a veterinarian."

Chuckling, he pulled his hand back and refastened the cuff at his wrist. "I'll feel more comfortable with Doc treating me. Regular doctors make me nervous."

"What about nurses?" she asked pointedly.

One corner of his mouth cocked upward. "Nurses unsettle me, too. Especially when she has a syringe and needle in her hand."

She showed him her empty palms. "I can't give you a tetanus shot. But I could clean those wounds for you," she offered. "I keep antiseptic and things like that in the coffee shop. Just in case I cut or burn myself."

"Thanks for the offer, but I'd rather just sit here and drink my coffee." He gazed around the shaded dining area, then across the street to where a fat saguaro shaded a small building that housed an insurance agency. "This is quiet. No bawling cows or nickering horses. Not that I don't like those sounds, but sometimes a man wants to just listen to the wind. And a woman's voice."

She cleared her throat and his gaze swung back to her. Emily-Ann was surprised to see the humor had disappeared from his face. In fact, if she didn't know better, he looked lonely, almost lost. Which hardly made sense. This man had everything going for him. He'd just landed a prestigious job as foreman of Three Rivers Ranch. Why should he be feeling anything but ecstatic? Unless he was missing some woman back in Texas, she thought.

"You forgot the coyotes," she said in an attempt to lighten the moment. "None of those howling around here. Although, they do show up in town once in a while."

He smiled and she was relieved to see his good humor returning. The other night at the party she'd been drawn to his easy, laid-back nature. It was a nice change from the guys she'd dated in the past who'd been so busy trying to play the cool, tough man that they'd rarely smiled. And even when they had, it had looked so phony she'd had to bite her tongue to keep from laughing.

"No. Can't forget them." He took the last bite of Bismarck, then wadded up the empty wax paper.

As Emily-Ann watched him tilt the foam cup to his lips, she realized she didn't want him to leave. Spending time with him made her feel different, almost special. She realized that was foolish. Especially since she'd believed her past mistakes with men had taught her some valuable lessons.

"So has anything exciting been going on at Three Rivers since the party?" she asked, then before he could answer, added, "I guess everything about the place must feel exciting and new to you."

"It does," he agreed. "Matthew has been trying to show me the different sections of the ranch and how they're used throughout the year. The majority of the land has to be explored on horseback. So we've been spending lots of time in the saddle."

"Camille implied that she and Matthew would be staying for a few more weeks. Maybe until the end of the month. I hope they do. Once they go back to Red Bluff I'll only get to see her occasionally."

"Matthew tells me that Camille owns and operates a little diner down there. I think he said the town was called Dragoon. Is that right?"

Emily-Ann nodded. "Yes. It's a tiny desert town. Not much is there, but the diner is located on the edge of a main highway that runs from Wilcox to Benson. So she has lots of travelers who stop in to eat."

"Hmm. Just between me and you, I'm surprised that Camille runs a diner." He shrugged. "Not that anything is wrong with running a diner. It's just that she's a Hollister. There's no need for her to work at such a strenuous job."

"You're right about no need. But her being a Hollister explains everything. In spite of their wealth, or maybe because of it, they all have a fierce ambition. Camille couldn't sit around and twiddle her thumbs any more than her brothers or sister, Vivian, could. Besides, she loves to cook and she's darned good at it. If you ever make a trip down to Red Bluff, you'll see what I mean."

"I plan to go for a visit later on in the year," he said. "Just to see how Matthew is putting that Hollister property to use."

"You know, Camille was a bone of contention for a while with her family. When she moved down to Red Bluff and refused to come back here, her brothers threw a fit, so to speak. And Maureen wasn't happy about it either," Emily-Ann told him. "But that's all been smoothed over now that she and Matthew have married and are going to have a baby soon. Funny how things can look so bleak for a while and then everything suddenly turns to sunshine again. Sort of gives a person hope. You know what I mean?"

Smiling faintly, he put down his cup and leaned back in the chair. "I know exactly what you mean. And everybody needs hope."

He was right. Everybody needed hope. But no one had ever clung to it as much as Emily-Ann's mother. She'd always looked forward and believed that the men in her life were actually going to come through with all their promises. In the end, Emily-Ann had ended up having no contact with her biological father and her stepfather had been little more than a stranger who'd come and gone as he pleased.

"Well, I need to be going," he said after a moment. "Doc is expecting me and I promised Matthew I'd be back to the ranch in time to go with him to check on some calves."

All sorts of words she wanted to say rushed to

her tongue. But none of them were appropriate or proper. Besides, she didn't want him to get the idea that she was gushing over him.

She gestured to his injured arm. "Promise me that you'll have Doc treat that bite wound. It could become seriously infected if you don't take care of it."

"I promise as soon as I leave here, I'm going straight to his clinic," he told her.

"Well, I'm glad you came by, Tag. Now that you know where the coffee shop is you might get a hankering to drop by for another pastry—sometime."

He looked across the table at her. "I expect I will. But before I go I have something else on my mind—to ask you."

That serious look had returned to his face and she wasn't sure what to make of him. Nor did she understand what had caused her heart to suddenly leap into a ridiculous tap dance. "Oh. What's that?"

"Would you be willing to have dinner with me? I can't tonight. But I think I'll be free tomorrow night—if you are."

Free? He couldn't possibly know just how long ago a man of any caliber had looked in her direction, much less asked her on a date.

"Uh—I'm not busy, if that's what you mean. But I—"

"But what?"

She frowned, unwilling to believe that this cowboy wanted to spend time with her. "Are you—would this be like a date?"

"I guess you could call it that. Why?"

She felt her jaw drop and she realized she was probably staring at him like she'd lost her senses.

"Well, you—uh, you said we were going to be friends."

"That's right. Friends can eat dinner together, can't they?"

She was growing more flustered by the second. "Yes. But friends don't go on dates."

A slow smile spread his lips and she found herself staring at his white teeth. What would it feel like to push her tongue past their rough edges? To taste his inner mouth and press her body so close to his that not even a hair could be wedged between them?

Oh Lord, she was already losing control, she thought desperately, and they'd not gone any farther than the front yard of the coffee shop.

He reached across the table and clasped his hand around hers. The contact caused her heart to thump even harder.

He said, "After we go on a date we might decide we want to be more than friends."

"No!"

His brows arched in question and before he could make any sort of reply, she tried to explain, "I mean—you don't know who I am, Tag."

"Why don't I? Your name is Emily-Ann Broadmoor. You work at this little coffee shop and you're studying to be a nurse. You've always lived in Wickenburg and you're not married or attached. Right?"

The sigh she released was rough and shaky. "Yes. But you don't understand. I'm not a girl that someone like you would want to date."

He appeared unaffected by her admission. "Why not?"

Annoyed with herself and with him, she pressed her lips together and shook her head. "Look, Tag, I know you're a smart guy, so don't insult my intelligence by playing dumb. There are social ladders, you know. And I'm on the bottom rung. Got it now?"

"No. I don't have it. You can't be a friend of the Hollisters and be on the bottom rung. That just isn't possible."

"The Hollisters see everyone as equal. And when two little girls become friends in elementary school—they don't care about such things. They just want to be together. And because of Camille, the Hollisters have always included me. It's not that way with everyone around here. And please don't ask me why. It's something I don't want to get into. Not now."

She rose from her chair and gathered the remnants of her snack from the tabletop. "I need to go back in and finish closing up," she told him.

He rose and, with his trash in hand, followed her into the building. After the door had shut behind them, he asked, "Would you like to know what I'm really thinking?"

Walking behind the counter, she began to sack up the last of the pastries. "Sure. Go ahead," she told him.

He tossed his trash into a nearby basket, then pulled out his wallet and placed several bills on the glass countertop.

"I think you're talking a lot of nonsense. If you're afraid to go out with me just come out and say it. That would be much better than you giving me all this double-talk about you not being good enough— or whatever it is you're trying to say."

She closed the doors on the back of the case and placed the last of the sacked pastries on a cabinet top that ran along the back wall of the room. Behind her, she could hear Taggart's boots shuffle restlessly against the tiled floor.

He was obviously waiting on her reply. But what could she say without lying? She was afraid to go out with him. Afraid she'd do something foolish like fall head over heels for him.

Turning, she walked over to where he was standing. "Okay. You're right. I am a little afraid to go out with you, Tag. I—you see, I haven't wanted to date anyone for a long time. It never turns out good for me. And to be honest, I like you too much to ruin things between us."

He shook his head. "Having dinner together isn't going to ruin anything."

Before she could stop it, a cynical laugh rushed past her lips. "That's what you think."

He grinned a charming little grin at her. "I promise I'll be a perfect gentleman."

She laughed again, only this time it was a sound of amusement. "I believe you."

"So does that mean you'll go?"

It was stupid for her to keep hesitating, she thought, when every cell in her body was screaming at her to accept his invitation.

"Yes, I'll go. I just don't understand why you're asking me. If you'll look around town you'll see there are all sorts of women who are much prettier than me."

"Maybe I want more than pretty," he said, then smiling smugly, he tapped a finger on the bills he'd placed on the countertop. "Here's the money for my things. I'll see you tomorrow night. About seven. Is that time okay with you?"

"Sure."

She scratched down her address on an order pad and handed the small square to him. "That's where I live. And I put my cell number below. Just in case you change your mind and need to call me."

He slipped the paper into the pocket on his Western shirt. "No chance I'll change my mind," he said, then tipping the brim of his hat at her, he left the shop.

After the door had closed, Emily-Ann let out a long breath and sank weakly onto the wooden stool sitting next to the cabinets.

This morning as she'd driven to work, she'd pretty much convinced herself that Taggart had put her out of his mind. Now she was going on a date with him. It was a bit unbelievable to Emily-Ann. And what was Camille going to think about it?

She wasn't going to tell her, Emily-Ann thought. Not yet. If she did, her friend would immediately start harping about that damned bridal bouquet again. No, she'd wait until the date was over and Taggart came up with a reason not to see her again. Then she'd have proof that she needed more than a bridal bouquet to find a man to love her.

Chapter Four

Taggart hadn't realized just how many things he'd accumulated until he started unpacking the boxes he'd brought with him from Texas. Dishes, bedding and bath linens, clothing, boots and toiletries. Each evening before he'd gone to bed, he'd tried to unpack at least one box and put the items where they belonged.

This evening Matthew had insisted they wrap up work early so he could finish getting his house in order. Now, as he stacked coffee cups and cereal bowls in one of the kitchen cabinets, he was interrupted by a knock on the front door.

Forgetting the task for the moment, he went out to the living room to answer the door.

"Blake, come in," he said, surprised to find the ranch manager standing on the wide wooden porch.

"I can just stay a minute. Mom and I are about to leave for Prescott to a cattle buyer's convention."

Taggart pushed the door wide and gestured for Blake to enter the house. "I was in the kitchen trying to put away the last of the dishes. This moving thing is a pain."

"I'd be happy to send Jazelle over here to help you. That is, if Katherine and Roslyn can make do without her. These days she's turned into more of a nanny than a housekeeper," he added with a chuckle. "Poor girl. Mom has decided she needs to hire someone to help her and I agree."

"Thanks for the offer, but I have most of the necessary things put where they belong. Come on back to the kitchen," Taggart told him. "We can talk while I finish with the dishes."

"Fine. This won't take long," Blake said, while following him through the living room. "Actually, I stopped by because I have something to give you."

Inside the kitchen, Taggart gestured toward a long white farm table with matching chairs. "Pull up a chair. I have a bit of coffee left in the carafe if you'd like a cup."

"Thanks. But I'm fine." He reached inside his

Western-cut jacket and pulled out a long envelope, then handed it to Taggart.

"What is this?" Taggart asked curiously.

"A check."

Taggart paused and looked in stunned fascination at the ranch manager. "What for? Are you terminating my job already?"

The question produced a long, loud laugh from Blake. "Not hardly. We couldn't be happier that we have you here. The check is a little bonus. Just to show how much we appreciate you. We understand it's been costly for you to move out here. Especially with you bringing horses and tack, besides your household goods and personal things. We want to help cover the expense."

"I don't expect that, Blake. And it's totally unnecessary." He opened the envelope and the amount of the check he pulled out very nearly floored him. "No! No way can I accept this. I didn't spend a fraction of this on moving cost."

Blake laughed again. "Don't argue. Just trust me. You'll earn it all back before the first month is out."

Shaking his head, Taggart said, "I don't know what to say. This is far beyond generous, Blake."

The ranch manager swatted a dismissive hand through the air. "No need for you to say anything about the check. But I would like to know how you're settling in. Not with the house, I can see things here are taking shape. I'm talking about the ranch and the men. You and Matthew have been so busy, I've not had a chance to talk with either one of you."

Taggart studied the eldest Hollister brother, while thinking how differently he was being treated here at Three Rivers compared to the last year he'd spent on the Flying W. No matter how hard he'd worked, the Armstrongs had never been satisfied. They'd demanded more from him and all the hands, all the while insisting they had to cut their wages or go under. Which the whole crew had known was utter nonsense. It had been a hellish situation and one that Taggart was glad to have behind him. "Everything is going good, Blake. Thank you for asking."

Blake gave his shoulder an affectionate slap. "That's what we want. But if you do have any problems of any kind I want you to feel comfortable about coming to me. Or Mom. She stays in the thick of things and knows more about this ranch than I'll ever learn in my lifetime. But you've probably already figured that out for yourself."

"Matthew told me what an incredible woman his mother-in-law is and I'm beginning to see he wasn't exaggerating. Today Maureen helped drag calves to the branding fire and I'm being honest, she outworked most of the men," Taggart replied.

"That's Mom," Blake said with a grin, then turned to go. "And speaking of Mom, she's probably waiting on me. I'll see you tomorrow."

"Uh, Blake, if you have another minute I would like to ask you something."

At the back door of the kitchen, Blake paused to look at him. "Okay. Shoot."

Feeling a bit foolish, he cleared his throat, then asked, "How well do you know Emily-Ann?"

If the question surprised Blake he didn't show it. In fact, he chuckled. "I thought you were going to ask me something about roundup."

"I'm not worried about roundup," Taggart told him.

Blake looked even more amused. "But Emily-Ann does worry you?"

"Not exactly worries me," Taggart tried to explain. "More like she confuses the heck out of me."

"I didn't realize you were interested in her."

Taggart could feel his cheeks growing warm. He never discussed women with anyone. Since he'd lost Becca, he'd never really thought that much about any particular female. But since he'd met Emily-Ann something had happened to him. He couldn't seem to get his mind off the curvy redhead or that kiss they shared the night of the party.

"I'm taking her out to dinner tonight," Taggart admitted, then with a helpless shake of his head, added, "To be honest, Blake, she came damned close to turning down my invitation. Which is her right, of course. I hardly expect just any and every woman to go out with me. But she—well, it's like she mistrusts me or something."

Blake grinned. "You must've done something right. She's agreed to go out with you. But as far as giving you advice about women, I'm not the right man for that job. You need to talk to Holt. He's the charmer of the family."

Taggart swiped a hand through his dark rumpled hair. "Go ahead and laugh, Blake. I realize I sound like I'm twenty years old instead of thirty-two. It's just that she puzzles me. She seems to have a low opinion of herself and I can't figure why. I thought you might clue me in about her."

Blake's grin quickly vanished. "I don't know that much about Emily-Ann's personal life, Tag. Except that it hasn't always been easy. She's had to deal with plenty of heartaches and hardships. But she's a good person and very hardworking. We all love her."

"Hmm. It's odd that you say that. She has the notion that you Hollisters just tolerate her because she's Camille's friend."

Blake muttered a curse. "That's not true at all," he said, then after a thoughtful moment added, "but I can see where she might see things that way. Feeling accepted doesn't always come easy for some people. Especially when they've been raised up hard. I figure Emily-Ann needs to move on from the stigma of her past. But that's a hard thing to do, too."

Taggart frowned. "What about her past?"

Blake shook his head. "That's something she'll have to tell you."

Blake let himself out and as the door shut behind him, Taggart thoughtfully picked up the check from the countertop.

The bonus was nearly half of the year's salary he'd made on the Flying W. The Hollisters' generosity was hard to believe, much less accept. He wasn't worth this kind of money.

Let's just say I know my limitations. And you're on the other side of the boundary.

Emily-Ann's words suddenly pushed their way into Taggart's thoughts and he wondered if her lack of money made her think there was a wall separating them. Or did her reluctance have something to do with a man? One that she'd loved and lost?

Taggart intended to find the answers to his questions.

With a critical eye, Emily-Ann studied herself in the dresser mirror. Throughout the day, she'd promised herself she wasn't going to fret over her appearance tonight. She'd told herself she wasn't going to agonize over what to wear or how to do her hair. Glamming herself up for Taggart would be foolish and futile. She couldn't turn a dandelion into a lovely rose.

Yet, in spite of all the self-lecturing, she'd taken pains to pick out a dress that flattered her complexion. And she'd done her hair three different times to get it to drape perfectly against her temple.

And why not, she asked herself. Futile or not, any normal girl would want to look her best when she went on a date with a man. Especially a man like Taggart.

Turning away from the mirror, she reached for the thin yellow cardigan lying across the foot of the bed. Even though it was April, and the days were hot, the nights cooled enough for a jacket. And since Taggart hadn't given her any hint as to where they might be eating, she had no idea if she'd be spending any time outdoors.

With the sweater thrown over one arm and her handbag in tow, she left the bedroom and walked out to the living room to wait for Taggart to arrive. As she took a seat on the couch, she wondered what he would think about her house.

What can he think, Emily-Ann? It's the same little bungalow your mother lived in when you were born. You've never gotten beyond its walls. Except for a few little road trips, you've never ventured outside Wickenburg. You have a small, modest life. Before the night is over he's going to see all of that for himself.

Emily-Ann was fighting against the disheartening voice in her head when she heard the sound of a vehicle pull up in the short driveway in front of the house.

She was struck with the urge to jump up and go meet him on the front porch, but she quickly told herself that she needed to behave in a dignified manner. He didn't need to see that she was chomping at the bit to welcome him. Besides, he needed to get a good look at the inside of her house. Just so he'd see the huge gap in their living conditions.

After a short moment, a knock sounded on the door and Emily-Ann tried to gather her composure as she went to answer it. But as soon as she pulled back the door and saw him standing across the threshold, everything inside her began to tremble.

"Hi, Emily-Ann."

"Good evening, Tag. Please come in." She pushed the door wider, then waited while he stepped past her and into the house before she shut it behind them.

"I don't suppose you had trouble finding the place," she said as he came to a stop in the middle of the small room. "Wickenburg isn't very large."

"No problem," he told her. "GPS wasn't going to let me make a wrong turn."

"Would you like to sit for a minute?" she asked gesturing toward an armchair. "Or are you ready to go?"

"Since we have plenty of time I'll sit a minute," he said.

Emily-Ann watched him sink into the armchair, then remove his Stetson and place it on his knee. She'd expected him to want to leave. Most men did once they saw her house. Not that it was cluttered or nasty. But the old furniture had seen better days and the flooring needed to be replaced.

"If you'd like something to drink I can make coffee," she offered. "Or I have soda."

"Thanks," he said, "but I'm fine."

Feeling more nervous than she could ever remember being, she sat down on the couch directly opposite of where he was sitting. As she smoothed her skirt over her knees, she could feel his gaze sliding over her and to know he was looking at her was enough to light a fire in her cheeks.

"So how—"

"I thought—"

They both spoke at the same time and then laughed.

"Sorry," Taggart told her. "You go first."

"I was only going to ask you how things are going on the ranch," she said, while thinking how terribly sexy he looked tonight. He was wearing a deep blue shirt with black diamond-shaped snaps down the front and on the cuffs. A bolo tie with a slide fashioned from black onyx hung loosely below the collar of his shirt. He looked dressed up without being too fancy. In fact, he looked exactly right.

"They're going great. Better every day, in fact."

"That's nice. I'm glad for you. And the Hollisters," she added. "Before you came, Blake and Maureen were very concerned about losing Matthew."

"Well, they haven't exactly lost him. He's just working a different property now."

"Yes. But this ranch in Yavapai County is the biggest one," she reasoned.

"I'm reminded of that every day I pull up in the ranch yard and see all the hands coming out of the bunkhouse. Back on the Flying W I maybe had to deal with a third of the amount of men that I do here. For the first day or two after I arrived, I felt daunted by the sheer size of everything."

"But now you're growing accustomed to it, I'm guessing."

"More and more every day," he replied, then glanced around the small room. "You have a homey little place here, Emily-Ann. I like it."

"You're being overly nice, Tag. And it isn't necessary. I'm sure you see plenty of things that need repairing or replaced. I do what I can, whenever I can."

He frowned at her. "I'm not being overly nice. This room feels lived-in and I'm sure the rest of the house does, too. And that's a nice feeling. It's something you can't fake."

"Well, the house is very old. I think it was built in the 1940s and had several different owners until my mother moved into it in 1990. I was born a few months later. Some of my friends often tell me I should move into an apartment building. That it would be more modern and I wouldn't have to worry about the upkeep. Which is true. But I wouldn't feel comfortable. Here I have a little yard and my neighbors aren't right on top of me."

He smiled. "I think you should tell your friends to mind their own business."

She let out a long breath. Maybe Taggart truly was different, she thought. Maybe he didn't care that her closet wasn't full of fancy clothes or her house needed repairs. Maybe he actually wanted to be with her just because she was Emily-Ann and no other reason.

Laughing softly, she said, "That's not a bad idea. Do you have everything moved into your house now?"

He chuckled. "Everything is inside the house, but that's about all I can say. I still have things piled here and there in boxes. But I'm a typical bachelor, Emily-Ann, I don't care if my bed is made or I have to dig my clothes out of a box. I have more important things to think about. But I like the house. It even has a little fireplace and a small patio out back."

"That's nice. Actually, I've never been inside the house," she admitted. "Camille and I used to ride horses by the place. But, of course, that was years before she and Matthew got together so we never stopped or anything. In fact, right after he went to work for Three Rivers Ranch, he was married to someone else. But his wife was—I'll just come out and say it—she was awful. You see, she was hollow on the inside. No substance at all. When she flew the coop I don't think anyone was surprised. Not even him."

By the time she stopped speaking she realized he was eyeing her closely. Embarrassed heat suddenly poured into her cheeks. "Oh my, I'm sorry, Tag. I'm running off at the mouth and sounding like the town gossip. But I—didn't mean it that way. It's just that I wanted you to know that—well, I think I should just shut up before I make myself look even worse."

Shaking his head, he smiled faintly. "You don't sound like a gossip—you were just telling me about the past. And actually I'm thinking how fortunate Matthew was to have a second chance at happiness."

Relieved that he understood, she nodded. "Yes, if only everyone could be that fortunate."

Suddenly restless, she rose to her feet and draped the light sweater over her bare shoulders. "If you're ready to go, I am," she told him.

"Sure." He rose from the chair and levered the hat back onto his head. "I've not said anything yet, but you look extra beautiful tonight, Emily-Ann."

Beautiful. The only time she ever heard that word and her name coupled together was when her mother spoke them. To hear Taggart call her beautiful filled her with pleasure. It also made her very wary.

She'd made the mistake of believing a man's pretty words before. She couldn't make those same missteps with Taggart. And yet with all of her heart she wanted to believe he was sincere.

"Thank you. Since you didn't say where we'd be going I hope my dress is suitable."

He stepped closer as he eyed the off-the-shoulder dress made of red calico printed with tiny yellow flowers. A matching belt cinched in the waist, while the tiered hem fluttered against her calves.

"The dress is perfect," he murmured. "I like it."

Oh my. His voice reminded her of cool water trickling over rough stones. And he smelled like a real man. One with strong hands, broad strong shoulders and a constitution to match.

"I'm glad," she said huskily, then clearing her throat, she purposely stepped away from him and retrieved her purse from an end table. "I'm ready."

As soon as the last words came out of her mouth, she very nearly laughed. She was far from ready to deal with the feelings that Taggart was creating inside her. But she wasn't going to shy away from him. For once in her life, she was going to believe, if just for one night, that she was good enough to have this man's respect.

Jose's, the restaurant Taggart had chosen, was located on the edge of town, where the empty desert stretched toward a far range of jagged mountains. The building was a rambling, hacienda type with stucco walls painted a pale turquoise and a red tiled roof. A deep porch ran the width of the front and was shaded with a roof supported by arched columns. Potted plants hung from the center of each arch, while an enormous bougainvillea covered with yellow-gold blossoms grew far past the roof. At the opposite end of the porch, a single saguaro with three arms stood against the darkening sky.

As Taggart and Emily-Ann walked across the graveled parking area to the building, he said, "I'm sure you've probably eaten here dozens of times. But Doc tells me the place has great food."

"To be honest, Tag, I'm rarely ever out this way. I usually just fix myself something at home. Or if I do decide to treat myself, I grab something close in town. This is very nice. And it's lovely here, don't you think?"

He looked down at her, while thinking nothing could look as lovely as she did at this moment with the twilight falling on her soft features and the smile on her face directed solely at him. He'd never known a woman as guileless as Emily-Ann and when he was with her, he forgot most everything. Even his vow to never let himself care for another woman.

"If the food is as good as the outside looks, then I think we're in for a treat," he told her.

Inside the restaurant, a hostess ushered them to a table covered with an orange-and-white checked tablecloth. In the center a fat brown candle flickered in the faint breeze wafting down from the blades of a ceiling fan. Beyond the small table, a long win-

dow exposed a view of the desert, while the sounds
of a Spanish guitar played softly in the background.

Taggart helped Emily-Ann into one of the cush-
ioned chairs, then took a seat for himself. All the
while it struck him that he could've driven for miles
and not found a more romantic spot than this. He'd
not exactly planned this type of dinner, but now that
they were here, and he saw the enchanted expression
on Emily-Ann's face, he was glad.

As soon as the waiter arrived, Taggart ordered
wine for each of them, then picked up the menu and
began to study the long list of dishes offered.

"I should've asked if you like Mexican food," he
said. "But I see they serve typical American food,
also."

"Oh, I love Mexican food," she exclaimed. "It's
my favorite. What about you?"

"Well, where I come from we had what you call
Tex-Mex food. It's a little different from the Mexican
food served here in Arizona, but it's just as good. I
like it all," he admitted.

"Do you eat in the bunkhouse with the men?" she
asked. "Or do you cook for yourself?"

"I do both. Depending on what I have planned in
the mornings or if I'm tied up late with work in the
evenings. The cook in the bunkhouse is a gruff old
guy. But he makes fairly good biscuits and beans
and steak. Blake eats in the bunkhouse, too, on certain days. I think he enjoys being a regular cowboy."

Emily-Ann nodded. "Blake went to college to get a degree in ranch management thinking one day when his dad grew old and retired he'd take over the job of manager. No one could've dreamed that Joel was going to die so young and that Blake would have to step into his father's position. Katherine, his wife, says that the job weighs on him at times, but he'll do whatever he has to do to keep the ranch thriving."

The waiter arrived with their drinks and after they'd given him their choices from the menu, Taggart took a long sip of the dry, fruity wine.

"Do you know Katherine well?" he asked, picking up on their conversation where they'd left off.

She nodded. "Yes. She comes by the coffee shop on the days that she's working at the school. She's secretary for Penny—the school principal."

"She and Blake seem like the perfect match."

"Perfect," she agreed. "Their twins are adorable. And their older son Nick is such a nice kid. Blake was the second of the Hollister men to get married. Joe, the deputy, was the first. I know you met him at the party."

Taggart had especially liked the youngest Hollister brother. "Yes, I did. He seemed like a quiet guy, but when his mother started talking about ranching, he really opened up. I got the impression that he does quite a bit of ranch work when he's off duty. By the way, he introduced me to Sam, foreman of the Bar X."

Emily-Ann gave him a huge smile. "Ahh, Sam. He's adorable."

"I've heard that women find him charming." He slanted her a wry smile. "I see that includes you, too."

Laughing softly, she drew the wineglass to her lips. "What can I say? His face looks like a piece of cracked and crinkled leather. He's as thin as a rail and his legs are just a little bowed. But there's something about that old man that—I don't know what it is. But women feel drawn to him. I think it's mostly that soft look in his blue eyes when he looks at us. Like he cherishes all females."

"Well, he's certainly snagged a nice one. Isabelle's mother rarely left Sam's side the night of the party. I hear they're going to get married."

Emily-Ann sighed and Taggart could see the starry expression in her eyes. She was clearly a romantic. But he'd come to that conclusion the first time he'd met her. So why had he brought her to dinner? Why was he here drinking wine with her and watching candlelight flicker golden fingers upon her bare shoulders?

Because you've lost your mind, Taggart. You've forgotten how it felt when you watched Becca being lowered into the ground. Because you can't remember what it was like to have every dream and hope you've ever carried in your heart crushed into bits of ashes.

No, damn it! He silently cursed at himself as he fought to block out the voice in his head. He hadn't forgotten anything. But he was determined not to allow the past to haunt him tonight. He was tired of remembering. Tired of living in the past and trying to hold on to a memory that only brought him pain.

"Honestly, I was shocked when I heard the news about Gabby and Sam," Emily-Ann replied. "I mean, yes, Sam is a charmer. And I have no doubt he'd treat a wife like a queen. But Gabby is so opposite from him. Besides the fact that she's probably twenty years younger and very attractive, she's a city person—an artist. Sam spends his days on the back of a horse."

Amused, he grunted. "What do you think I do?"

"The same thing. But I figure you're—" pausing, she made a palms-up gesture "—more of a well-rounded man than Sam."

"Hah! Don't kid yourself. I got the impression that Sam has already forgotten more than I'll ever know about anything. And sometimes it's that stark difference in people that make them attracted to each other." He leveled a smile at her. "But that's enough about those folks. What about you, Emily-Ann? How many hearts around here have you broken?"

Above the rim of the wineglass, her eyes made a slow study of his face. "Seriously? You have the idea that I've broken a heart?" Laughing cynically, she lowered the glass back to the table, but her fingers continued to grip the stem. "That's funny, Tag."

"Why?"

Frustration tightened her features. "Because— I'm not a girl who men fall in love with. That's why."

He frowned at her. "That's nonsense."

"I'm sorry," she said. "But it's true."

"You'll never convince me."

As he watched her lips curve into a wan smile he tried to imagine another man kissing her mouth, feeling her warm breath on his face, tasting the smooth skin of her cheek. But the image refused to form in his mind. Not because she was undesirable; everything about her was alluring. No, it was impossible to imagine her with another man because he was already thinking of her in possessive terms. As his and his alone.

The faint smile on her face suddenly vanished and she let out a short, mocking laugh before turning her gaze to the window. "Oh yes, you'll be convinced. You'll soon learn that I talk too much, that I'm irritating and sometimes even ditzy. I'm a bit plump for most men's taste and my mouth is too wide. My eyes are too big and I couldn't grow a long fingernail if I tried."

He could see she was deadly serious, but Taggart couldn't help himself, he had to laugh. "Oh, Emily-Ann, do you realize how ridiculous all of that sounds?"

Her gaze returned to his face and the cynicism

Taggart spotted in her green eyes took him by surprise.

"Yes, I can admit that most of it is trivial stuff,"
she said sullenly. "But that doesn't change the fact
that I'm Emily-Ann Broadmoor. Everyone knows my
father was the real estate tycoon's son. The one who
believed he was too high-class to marry the poor girl
he'd gotten pregnant. Too important to be a father to
the child she bore, or to ever acknowledge he had a
daughter. And I'm no different than my mother, Tag.
I'm the girl the guys want to take to bed, but never
fall in love with!"

By the time she spoke the last few words her voice
was wobbling and her face had turned to the color
of paste. The dark pain in her eyes was like a knife
in his chest and he desperately wanted to round the
table and take her into his arms. He wanted to tell
her in so many ways how very precious she was to
him. But that would be the same as saying he was
falling for her. He wasn't ready for that. And from
the sound of things, she wasn't either.

"Emily-Ann, I—"

His words were suddenly interrupted as she
jumped to her feet and blinked at the tears filling her
eyes. "I'm sorry, Tag. I—you'll have to excuse me."

She hurried away from the table and for a moment Taggart thought she might run from the restaurant completely. Relief rushed through him when
he saw her turn in the direction of an alcove where

the restrooms were located. Clearly, she was seeking a private space to collect herself. He could only hope she wouldn't allow this little episode to ruin their evening.

Sighing heavily, he reached for his wineglass and emptied it with one long swallow. Her emotional revelation had shaken him. Not because they were in a public place. And certainly not because he'd learned she'd been born out of wedlock. Nowadays no one looked down on a woman for being a single mother. Most of the time it was because she'd chosen to parent the child alone rather than enter into a marriage that wouldn't work. No, the part about her lack of a father hadn't meant that much to Taggart. Hell, for the majority of Taggart's childhood his father had been absent and now that he'd grown into adulthood he saw the man even less.

No, the part of Emily-Ann's admission that had cut Taggart so deeply was the last part. The part about being used instead of loved. Is that how she viewed most men? Did she put him in that same category? The idea sickened him.

Where do you come off being so righteous, Taggart O'Brien? Isn't that exactly what you've been thinking about Emily-Ann? You don't want love or marriage. But when you look at her, you definitely imagine having sex with her. You're no better than the rest. If you had any gumption about you at all you'd take her home and never see her again. And

*maybe, eventually, she'll meet a real man who'll give
her real love.*

Sighing heavily, he wiped a hand over his face,
then stared out the window at the darkening desert.
He'd asked Emily-Ann to have dinner with him tonight because in spite of the great job he'd just landed
at Three Rivers, and the money it was bringing to
him, he wanted more than that. She made him feel
alive again. She made him feel like a man.

He couldn't give her up now. But how did he think
he could hold on to her when the very thing she
wanted from a man he no longer had? His heart was
buried back in Texas.

Chapter Five

By the time Emily-Ann returned to the table, she had pulled her emotions together, but that didn't stop her from feeling like a complete fool. And when Taggart rose to his feet and promptly reached for her hand, she wanted to burst into tears all over again.

"I'm so sorry, Tag," she said lowly. "I hope I didn't embarrass you."

He smiled at her and the warm light in his brown eyes was more comforting to her than he could possibly know.

"What's embarrassing about your date going to the ladies' room? Everything is fine. I've ordered more wine and the waiter said our food should be arriving any minute."

He pulled out her chair and helped her into it as though nothing had happened. Emily-Ann couldn't possibly guess what he was actually thinking, but he was certainly making it easy to face him after the emotional debacle she'd pulled.

After he'd settled back into his own chair, she looked across the table at him. "Thank you, Tag. And I promise there won't be any more hysterics tonight."

"Forget it." He leveled an empathetic look at her. "To be honest, I'm glad you told me everything that you did. I understand you a little better now. There for a while I thought you didn't like me all that much."

She laughed and her reaction put a happy smile on his face. *Thank God*, she thought. Before she returned to the table, she was afraid he'd probably clamp a hand around her arm and lead her straight outside to his truck. And she wouldn't have blamed him. No man wanted to deal with an overwrought woman on their first date.

"I like you, Tag—a whole lot. And that outburst I had, it had nothing to do with you," she said, then promptly shook her head. "Well, that's not true. It had everything to do with you. Because I kept thinking I was ashamed for you to know about my life—my family. I thought you wouldn't want to be with me."

He reached across the table and squeezed her fingers. "I'm sorry that you ever thought such a thing. None of it makes any difference, Emily-Ann. I mean, I hate that your mother had her problems. But you know what I see when I look at you?"

She tightened her fingers around his. "No. Tell me."

"I see that your mother did a good job of raising her daughter."

She felt a part of her heart melting and she blinked her eyes as more tears threatened to appear. "That's the nicest thing anyone has ever said to me, Tag," she murmured. "I'll never forget it."

He started to reply, but the waiter suddenly arrived with their dinner, putting an end to the intimate moment. Still, Emily-Ann didn't mind the timing of the interruption. The night had just begun and she'd already stored away a lot of memories with this special man.

When Emily-Ann and Taggart left Jose's, the night had cooled drastically and she draped the sweater she'd carried with her around her bare shoulders and buttoned the top button to hold it in place.

Taggart understood she needed protection from the cold, but throughout their meal, he'd loved the sight of her bare shoulders. She had that creamy complexion that most redheads possessed and the freckles that dotted the bridge of her nose and cheekbones also speckled her shoulders. Several times during dinner, he'd caught himself fantasizing about kissing all those tiny brown dots and wondering if they were on other parts of her body.

But the fantasy of making love to Emily-Ann was not something he could act upon. The last thing he wanted was for her to think that this time he was spending with her was a prelude to sex. Still, none of that stopped him from resting his hand against the small of her back as they walked slowly to his truck. And to his relief, she didn't move away.

"It's still early. Would you like to take a drive out on the desert?" he asked, as he helped her into the passenger seat.

"I'd love to," she answered. "There's some interesting scenery to the west. But you're the driver, you choose."

"West it is."

After he'd settled himself behind the steering wheel, Taggart drove away from the parking lot and turned onto a street that would eventually lead them to a main highway.

"I've not been in this direction yet," he said once the city of Wickenburg began to appear in the rearview mirror. "I've mostly just driven the highway between town and Three Rivers."

"It's pretty in any direction," she commented, then asked. "Have you ever been to Prescott or Phoenix?"

"No. But sooner or later, I'm sure I'll be going for one reason or another. Actually, Maureen and Blake were going to Prescott tonight for some sort of cattle buyer gathering."

"And they didn't ask you to go with them?"

He grinned. "No, thank goodness. I think they're taking pity on me because we've been so busy. And spring roundup is about to start. That keeps everyone tied down for a week or more."

"I'm glad you didn't have to go to the meeting."

He said, "I'm glad, too. But I feel a little guilty. The Hollisters gave me a huge bonus check today. It was a total surprise. To be honest, the amount of it blew me away."

"You don't think you deserved it?" she asked.

"Not yet." He grunted with wry disbelief. "Heck, I'm not worth that kind of money."

"I don't think you've quite yet absorbed the huge job you've taken on. But the Hollisters do and they clearly appreciate you and trust that you're going to do things right."

"Yeah, I suppose. But I felt very undeserving." He glanced over to see she was studying him with an earnest expression. The idea that she was interested in his job and that she cared enough to discuss it with him not only surprised him, it drew him to her in a way he'd not expected.

"That's the way I felt when you asked me out to dinner," she said. "Very humbled."

"Oh, Emily-Ann. I don't ever want you to feel that way. Not about me or anything else."

From the corner of his eye, he could see she was smiling at him.

"I don't ever want you to feel that way, either," she said. "So we're even."

After traveling several more miles westward on the lonely strip of asphalt, a large picnic area appeared on the right side of the highway. Three concrete tables and a trash receptacle were positioned among two tall saguaros and several Joshua trees. At the moment there didn't appear to be anyone around. In fact, there wasn't any kind of light suggesting civilization was anywhere nearby.

"Let's stop and stretch our legs," he suggested.

"Sounds nice."

He parked the truck to one side of the graveled area and helped Emily-Ann down from the truck. The night had grown even colder than when they'd left Jose's and she quickly pushed her arms into the sweater.

"If it's too chilly for you we can get back inside the truck," he suggested.

"Not at all. It feels good."

Anchoring a hand on the side of her waist, he guided her forward past the tables and over to one of the Joshua trees. To the north of them a ridge of mountains jutted upward toward the starlit sky.

"This is beautiful," he said.

She asked, "I know you said Three Rivers's property looks different than the Flying W where you used to work. But what about this area? Does it look anything like your old stomping ground in Texas?"

"No. The only thing similar is the vast openness."

"Did it snow there?"

"Yes. Sometimes we even had blizzards. That's when ranching is especially hard work."

She looked up at him. "It rarely ever snows here. But that's okay. I'm a terrible driver on slick roads."

Icy fear suddenly lodged in his throat and he outwardly shivered as he tried to swallow away the sensation.

"Tag? Are you okay?"

He wiped a hand over his face. "Yeah, sure. I was just thinking that you should always be careful when you're driving. I lost someone I cared about to a car accident. I don't want anything to happen to you."

"Oh."

As her gaze continued to slip over his face, he could see all sorts of questions in her eyes and Taggart prayed that she wouldn't quiz him. Someday he would tell her everything. But not tonight. Not when he was beginning to feel a change coming over him. A change that he desperately needed.

"Then I promise I'll be extra careful from now on," she said, then with a cheerful smile, changed the subject completely. "See that area to the north? Where the mountains are in the far, far distance?"

He followed the line of her pointed finger. "Yes."

"That's where lots of gold was found in the Congress Mine back in 1884. A town by the same name boomed there for many, many years. But hardly anything is there now. And Constellation, another nearby mining town, is more or less a ghost town. Maybe you'd like to see them sometime? That is, if you like that sort of history. To me it's fascinating to think of all that sudden wealth and how it affected people back in those days when there was very little law and not much civilization."

"I'm sure there were a few men who were murdered for their gold," he said thoughtfully, then glanced down at her. "I would like to see the area sometime if you'd be willing to show me around."

"I'd like that," she said, then laughed. "Actually, one of the women who works at Chandler's clinic lives at Congress. And in her spare times she likes to pan for nuggets. Maybe we could hike up one of the canyons and try it. A good-sized nugget nowadays would buy new flooring for my living room."

He laughed. "That's a practical thought. But only one nugget would be enough?"

"I'm not greedy. Acquiring wealth never really was that important to me. Except…"

When her words trailed away, he looked down to see she was gazing wistfully out at the dark desert.

"Except what?"

"Oh, there were many times when my mother was alive that I wished I could have given her things and made her life easier. I did what I could, but I wish I could've done more." She turned her gaze up to his face. "Do you ever feel like that about your mother?"

He tried not to let the emptiness inside him show on his face. His mother had been the only real anchor he'd ever had in his life. When he'd lost her, it was like he'd drifted out in a big rough ocean with no way to swim back to shore.

"I used to. Before she died." His sigh could barely slip past the achy lump in his throat. "When Blake gave me the bonus check today, I couldn't help but think about her. She would've been amazed and proud. I wanted to change things for the better in her life, too. But her heart gave out before I had the chance."

She reached for his hand and, as the warmth of her fingers tightened around his, a sweet sort of contentment poured through him. The sensation was like nothing he'd ever felt and he wondered if he would ever experience it again. Or was this night something out of the ordinary and tomorrow all the magical feelings would vanish with the light of day?

"At first I didn't think the two of us had much in common," she said softly. "But I'm beginning to see that isn't entirely true."

With his hand still entwined with hers, he turned so that he was facing her. "We do have things in common and the best one is that we like each other's company. Don't we?"

She let out a long breath as her fingers tightened ever so slightly on his. "Yes, we do."

His free hand lifted and he touched the hair that framed part of her forehead. "You're a special woman, Emily-Ann. I want you to always remember that. Promise me that you will."

Starlight illuminated her face enough for him to see her lashes flutter and then her gaze latched on to his. The contact caused his stomach to clench.

"I promise," she whispered.

He allowed his fingers to drop to her cheek and as the tips moved ever so slightly against her petal-soft skin, he knew the rest of her would feel just as incredibly smooth.

"Emily-Ann," he said softly, "would you mind if I kissed you?"

Her gaze continued to cling to his and what he saw there caused his heart to hammer. She wanted him. Maybe just as much as he wanted her.

"I'd be disappointed if you didn't."

He drew in a sharp breath and then before he could change his mind or analyze the wisdom of his actions, he bent his head and softly placed his lips over hers.

She tasted just as good as she had the night of the party, yet somehow he managed to keep his passion tempered throughout the short kiss. Not for anything did he want her to get the idea that he had sex and only sex on his mind.

"That was nice," he murmured as he nuzzled her cheek with the tip of his nose. "Very nice."

Her tongue came out to nervously moisten her bottom lip. "Yes, it was. But I think we—uh, should head home now. I have an early morning scheduled and I'm sure you do, too."

In other words she wasn't going to give him, or herself, a chance to let a second kiss carry them away.

Well, that was good, Taggart thought. That was exactly how it needed to be. Until he was sure that she trusted him. Moreover, that he could trust himself.

"You're right. We should be getting back to your place. I have to meet Matthew at the cattle barn at five thirty in the morning."

His hand still on hers, he gently turned her in the direction of the truck. As they walked slowly back to the vehicle, he was acutely aware of her hip brushing against the side of his leg and the flowery scent of her hair drifting up to his nostrils. Over the years, he'd forgotten all the little things that made a woman enticing. Having Emily-Ann so close was a reminder of all that he'd been missing as a man and he wondered how long he'd be able to keep his desire reined in and his common sense intact.

When Taggart entered the cattle barn early the next morning, Matthew hadn't yet arrived. But he found Chandler busy wrapping up a C-section on a young cow. Since the two ranch hands that were trying to assist him were inexperienced with the process, they were both relieved to see Taggart.

"Boy, are we glad to see you, Tag," Jerry, the taller of the two men told him. "Me and Flip are trying to take care of this little guy, but we've never done this before."

While Chandler continued to stitch the cow's uterus back together, Taggart squatted over the newborn calf that was lying on a special bed to keep it warm. The mucus had already been cleaned from his nose and the rest of his body dried of afterbirth.

"He isn't struggling to breathe and you have him dry and warm. Looks like you've done things right so far," he told the two men.

"Yeah, but Doc says we'll have to see that he gets his mama's milk in the next couple of hours. That ain't gonna be easy," Flip said.

"Easy or not, the calf needs his mother's colostrum," Taggart told the men. "If the mother doesn't want to nurse we'll have to change her mind."

He turned back to Chandler, who'd already moved on to stitching the incision in the cow's flank.

"How is she, Doc?" Taggart asked.

Not bothering to look up, Chandler continued to stitch. "She'll be fine. And the calf doesn't appear to be too stressed. Hopefully, he'll stand within the hour."

Taggart glanced over at the black calf. "He looks big."

"Hell yes, he's far too big for this girl to give birth the normal way. I've been telling Blake the bull he has on this bunch of heifers is too large. I hope you can convince him to do something about it."

"He wants big healthy calves," Jerry spoke up in Blake's defense.

Chandler frowned at the ranch hand. "What good is that going to do if the mamas die trying to give birth to them?"

"I'll talk to him about it," Taggart assured Chandler. "But I'm not sure I'm the right person to convince him."

Chandler muttered a curse as he tied off the suture and poured antiseptic over the incision. "You're the foreman, Tag. It's your job to give him advice about the cattle."

"I know, but Blake is—"

"Not some sort of ranching god," Chandler insisted. "He's just the manager. He doesn't know everything."

Taggart heard shuffling feet behind him and looked over his shoulder to see Jerry and Flip exchanging amused glances. They might think it funny to hear Chandler say Blake didn't know everything. But Taggart hardly found it amusing. He didn't want to get caught in a war of wills between the two brothers.

Taggart said, "I'll talk to him about the bull. If Blake is agreeable to the idea, we could exchange him with the one on the Buzzard Gap range. He's nicely built but a bit smaller."

"Good choice," Chandler said.

With his job finished, the vet gathered his tools and medications, then turned his attention to the calf. Taggart joined him and watched closely as Chandler checked the calf's vitals.

"Thank God his respiration is good." Hanging the stethoscope around his neck, he rose to his full height. "I wish TooTall was here. He's a wizard with calves like this."

"TooTall? Is he a ranch hand I haven't met?" Taggart asked.

"He's Matthew's foreman down on Red Bluff. They're also the best of friends. I don't know if it's because TooTall is Yavapai or what, but he understands livestock and instinctively knows how to care for them. As for this little guy, I'll have to leave him in your hands, Tag. I've got to get to the clinic, pick up Trey and be at the Rafter R Ranch by six thirty. And considering that place is twenty minutes west of Wickenburg, I'm going to be late."

Chandler started out of the barn in a long stride and Taggart called after him, "Don't worry. Doctors are never on time. And put the calf out of your mind. I'll see that he's taken care of."

* * *

It wasn't until the end of the day, after Taggart and Matthew had ridden back into the ranch yard, that Tag had a chance to stop by Blake's office.

Since he'd started working at Three Rivers, which had been about three weeks ago, he'd only been in the ranch manager's office a handful of times. He was already learning that his secretary, Flo, a redhead in her late sixties, had a louder bark than she did bite, and that Matthew and Holt were two of her pets.

Now, as Taggart stepped into the outer office where her desk was located at one end of the long room, the secretary peered over the tops of her bifocals at him.

"Hello, Tag. How's it going today?"

He took a moment to walk over to the woman's desk. So far he'd never seen the work space anywhere close to being tidy. Papers and envelopes, manila folders, and all types of pens and pencils were scattered across the desktop, along with several coffee mugs. Among the jumble was an up-to-date computer and monitor, but so far he had yet to see her using it.

"Busy. Very busy," he told her. "What about you?"

"It never lets up. And at this time of the year Holt gives me the task of filling out all the registration papers for the new foals." Tapping a pencil against the desktop, she regarded him with a thoughtful gaze. "Are you enjoying Three Rivers Ranch so far?"

"I am. The Hollisters are good people."

"You got that right," she said, then sighed. "I miss the heck out of Matthew, but he just had to go and get himself married. Good for him, but just terrible for my heart."

She laughed then and Taggart chuckled with her.

"I hope you're not thinking about getting married yet, Tag. I'm beginning to like you and I'd hate to see you go, too."

Him married? Before his mind could scoff away that idea, Emily-Ann was pushing her way into his thoughts. Not that she'd ever been that far away. All day long she'd been lurking at the edges of his mind, making it hard for him to focus.

"Rest easy, Flo. I don't have any kind of plans for matrimony. And even if I did, I wouldn't leave Three Rivers."

He was about to ask her if Blake was still in his office when a door leading into the man's private office opened and Blake stuck his head around the wooden panel.

"Flo, is—" He paused as he spotted Taggart standing in front of the secretary's desk. "Tag! I didn't know you were here. Did you stop by to see me or Flo?"

Taggart grinned at the secretary. "Well, Flo is much prettier than you. But I'm not sure she wants to talk about cows."

Flo batted a dismissive hand at the two men. "You two go talk about cows. I have work to do."

Blake motioned for Taggart to join him and he followed the ranch manager into his private office.

The room was furnished with plush leather furniture and decorated with all sorts of photos taken from different sections of the ranch. Some of them depicted huge herds of horses, while others were images of cattle grazing on desert mountain slopes and along the river's edge.

"Would you like some coffee? It's only two hours old," Blake said with a chuckle. "But I can have Jazelle bring us some fresh."

"Don't bother with that. I'm fine." He started toward one of the wooden chairs in front of Blake's desk, but detoured at the last moment when one particular photo on the wall caught his eye. It was a picture of a very old cabin shrouded by cottonwoods, pines and blooming sagebrush. "This is neat. I'm guessing it must be on the ranch somewhere."

"It's the original Three Rivers Ranch house. That's where my great great grandparents lived when they first arrived in Yavapai County."

Taggart was amazed. All along he'd assumed that the Hollisters had always had wealth. Obviously this photo proved that theory wrong.

"Are you saying the ranch started like this and grew into what it is today? That's incredible, Blake." He turned away from the photo to see Blake was sitting in the executive chair behind his desk. The wan smile on his tired face held a touch of pride.

"I agree. Sometimes I have to stop and remind myself that the ranch wasn't always like this." He shrugged one shoulder. "Actually, I think my great great grandfather came to Arizona planning to find a fortune in gold. But he didn't take to mining and soon figured out he could make money by raising beef to feed all the miners and people who'd flooded in to the area in search of wealth. And as it turned out, he figured right. The gold ran out, but the need for beef still remains."

Taggart sank into one of the chairs and propped his ankles out in front of him. He'd had a long day and it wasn't over yet. But when he listened to Blake talk about his ancestors and the beginning of the ranch, he realized that he'd become a part of something bigger than he could've ever imagined. It was a heady feeling for the little boy who'd once worn hand-me-down clothes and helped his mother stuff rags around the window facings to keep the dust and cold wind from blowing into their house.

"The man obviously had a vision," Taggart remarked.

"Yeah. And sometimes not following the crowd takes courage," Blake said, then lifted a brow in his direction. "But you didn't come by to talk about the history of the Hollisters and Three Rivers. What's on your mind?"

"Bulls. And calves," he said bluntly. "Chandler had to perform another C-section this morning. The fourth one out of that particular head of heifers. I understand that four is a mighty small number when you're dealing with thousands, but the way I see it, each cow and calf is important."

"Damn right each one is important." He swiped a hand over his face. "I haven't had a chance to talk to Chandler today. Is the cow/calf pair okay?"

Taggart nodded. "The cow is in fine shape. The calf is a little weak, but he's coming around. I have Flip and Jerry caring for him."

Blake's brows pulled together in a frown. "And that's two men you could use elsewhere."

"I'm not concerned about being shorthanded."

"Then you're worried that more C-sections are going to be needed." He rose from the chair and walked over to a small table holding a coffee maker and all the fixings. After he poured himself a cup of the black liquid, he carried it over to a long leather couch and sank onto the end cushion. "Last year I took a chance and put Rambler—that's the bull on Juniper Flats—on that particular herd of heifers. Every rancher wants big healthy calves and I was hoping there wouldn't be problems. Looks like I made the wrong choice."

"I wouldn't say you made the wrong choice," Taggart reasoned. "A man has to take chances if he ever expects to get what he wants."

Grimacing, Blake sipped the coffee. "True. But in this case it looks like I need to make another choice."

Taggart shifted uncomfortably on the chair. "I'd like to make a suggestion. That we move the bull that's presently on the Buzzard Gap range to the heifers' pasture. His size would be much more compatible. I think it would cut down on the number of difficult births."

Blake leveled a knowing look at him. "You've been talking to Chandler about this."

"Only this morning when he was finishing up the surgery. But if you're thinking I'm here to be Doc's voice, you're wrong. I'm speaking for the welfare of the heifers and babies."

"Well, I'll tell you, Tag, Mom and I hired you because of your experience and knowledge. We value and welcome your opinion."

While Blake leaned back against the couch and thoughtfully considered the situation, Taggart rubbed a hand against the stubble on his jaw. His face hadn't seen a razor since last night, before he'd picked up Emily-Ann. But he'd never liked shaving and avoided the task as long as he could. If he looked grungy now, he doubted the ranch manager cared.

"All right, Tag, I'm going to go along with your suggestion. Even though part of the breeding season has already taken place, it might save us problems on down the line."

More relieved than he cared to admit, Taggart

thanked him and the two men went on to discuss how and when to move the bulls. Once everything was decided, Taggart stood.

"I've taken up enough of your time," Taggart told him, then glanced at his watch. "You've probably missed dinner with your family."

Blake chuckled. "The twins are always waiting to join me, so their daddy never eats alone," he said. "And speaking of dinners, how did yours go with Emily-Ann last night?"

With everything Blake had to deal with, Taggart hadn't expected Blake to remember about the date with Emily-Ann, much less ask about it.

"It was good. I enjoyed it and I think she did, too."

Blake nodded with approval. "Glad to hear it. She deserves a nice guy like you."

She certainly deserved a nice guy, Taggart silently agreed. But he could hardly put himself in that category. Not when half of his thoughts about Emily-Ann were far from nice. In fact, they were downright naughty.

Clearing his throat, Taggart said, "Emily-Ann deserves the best. But I—I'm not really in the market for anything serious."

Crossing his arms across his chest, he studied Taggart for a long moment. "Dear God, don't tell me you're like Holt used to be."

"How's that?" Taggart asked.

Blake snorted. "Too many women and not enough

time. That was Holt's motto—until he met Isabelle.
I didn't know a man could be that transformed until
I saw it with my own eyes."

Taggart was as far from a womanizer as a man
could get. And he sure couldn't picture himself as
a husband or daddy. Not now. With a shake of his
head, he said, "I don't think I need to be transformed.
Not like Holt."

Laughing, Blake shooed him toward the door.
"You must be tired. Get on out of here."

Taggart left the office and as he shut the door behind him, he saw Flo still working diligently over a
ledger book. Did people still use those things? Apparently, she did.

Not bothering to glance up, Flo said, "I heard
laughter. You must have said something really funny
to make Blake laugh."

"Just a little something about my love life, Flo."

That brought her head up and as she stared at
him with her mouth open, Taggart hurried out of
the office.

Chapter Six

"Oh, look at that yellow-print dress! It's adorable!" Camille exclaimed as she and Emily-Ann paused on the sidewalk to peer in the plate glass window of Cactus and Candles Boutique. "You would look great in it!"

Emily-Ann groaned. "I don't have the waistline for that. But you do."

"Don't be silly. You have curves from here to yonder and the belt at the waistline will show them off. Now me, I have no waist at all right now."

"Well, not at the moment," Emily-Ann told her as she eyed Camille's very pregnant belly. "But you'll have one soon. Come on, let's go in and you buy the dress for yourself. It'll look great with a pair of cowboy boots."

Laughing, Camille grabbed her by the hand and the two women went into the little boutique.

An hour later, they came out with Emily-Ann carrying two sacks filled with dresses, shoes and fashion jewelry.

"You shouldn't have bought these things for me," Emily-Ann continued to argue as she loaded the items into the back seat of Camille's truck. "I thought we came out this afternoon to spend time together, not your money."

"Oh, pooh, I didn't spend that much. And if I can't buy my friend something once in a while, then what good is having money?" Camille said as she slipped behind the steering wheel. "Besides, do you know how often I go shopping for girly things?"

"I doubt very often," Emily-Ann said as she climbed into the passenger seat and fastened her seat belt. "From what you say, you're usually at the diner, or working on the baby's nursery. And what about that sweet little tot you're carrying? There's a children's store on the next block. It has all sorts of clothing and toys and baby furniture. Let's go in there and I'll pick out something for him."

"Whoa, did you say *him*?"

Emily-Ann grinned. "I did. A boy is what I think it's going to be. Why? Do you or Matthew want a girl?"

Smiling, Camille reversed the truck onto the street. "Well, I think a girl would be nice. After all, I have four brothers and only one sister. As for Matthew, it doesn't matter to him. I think he's already got it in his head that we're going to have a dozen babies."

"Uh, that might be kind of hard on you, don't you think?"

Camille laughed. "Well, twelve was kind of an exaggeration on my part. But I know he wants at least two or three children and so do I."

Emily-Ann looked over at her friend. "I can't imagine how you must feel, Camille. To have Matthew love you like he does and to know you're going to have his baby. You must feel like you're floating on a cloud or something."

Spotting the sign of the children's store hanging beneath the awning over the sidewalk, Emily-Ann pointed to an empty parking spot. "There's the store. Pull in here."

Camille parked the truck, but kept the motor and the air-conditioning running as she turned on the seat to look at Emily-Ann. "Before we go in I want to say something about your floating-on-a-cloud idea. Marriage isn't a big party where everything is fun and perfect."

Emily-Ann grimaced. "I might be scatterbrained at times, but I have sense enough to know that nothing in life is perfect. Including people and marriages.

God knows I had to watch Mom suffer through years of a worthless husband. But you're very happy, Camille. And you do have a man who loves you."

"You're right on both counts. But that doesn't mean every day is smooth sailing. I'm busy trying to keep the diner a profit, while planning for the baby. And Matthew is working long hours to build up Red Bluff. But," she added with a dreamy grin, "we're doing it all together. And that makes everything worthwhile."

Shaking her head, she said, "If you're trying to give me marriage advice, Camille, you're wasting your time. It's going to take more than your bridal bouquet to find me a good man. It'll take a miracle."

Camille reached over and pressed Emily-Ann's hand between both of hers. "This life I have with Matthew—that's what I want for you, Emmie. To have someone who loves you. Someone you can share the good and bad times with. I know it will happen for you if you just let it."

The image of Taggart's handsome face suddenly floated to the front of Emily-Ann's mind, yet to imagine a man such as him loving her, sharing his life with her seemed impossible.

Three days had passed since he'd taken her to Jose's for dinner and she'd not seen or heard from him even once. But that discouraging fact wasn't enough to get the man's kiss out of her mind. And he had kissed her. Oh yes. The memory of when they'd stood beneath the Joshua tree and he'd pulled her into his arms was still achingly fresh in her mind. But apparently it had been a forgettable moment for him. Otherwise, he would have surely contacted her by now.

Determined not to let Taggart O'Brien ruin this evening with her friend, she purposely put on a cheery face. Not for anything did she want Camille to guess that she was pining foolishly over something she couldn't have.

"I'll try to let it happen. And maybe one day it will. Right now I'm just thrilled for you," she said, then tugged on her hand. "Now come on. Let's go buy the kid something he can have fun with later on."

Camille laughed. "You're saying *he* again. I might as well give up and accept the fact that we're going to have a son. That's what TooTall has been saying all along anyway. And you can't argue with that guy's predictions."

"Oh yes. TooTall is the mystic Yavapai. The one who kept telling Matthew he was going to marry you." She thoughtfully tapped a finger against her chin. "Wonder what kind of prediction he'd make for me?"

"Hmm. Probably that once you become a nurse you're going to fall in love and marry a handsome doctor."

Emily-Ann burst out laughing. "I wouldn't take a doctor if you handed him to me on a silver platter. If he wasn't working, he'd always have his patients on his mind. Just give me a good ole Joe. Preferably, one with a heart."

Rolling her eyes, Camille cut the motor and reached for her handbag. "You know what's wrong with you, Emmie? When it comes to men you're just too picky."

Laughing again, Emily-Ann opened the truck door. "Come on. Let's see if we can find junior a pair of miniature chaps like his daddy wears."

By the time Taggart left Hollister Animal Clinic and pulled into Emily-Ann's driveway, it was nearing eight thirty. He doubted she would be in bed at such an early hour, but he also realized it was rather late to make an unexpected visit. But three days had passed since their date and he'd waffled about contacting her. If she slammed the door in his face, he couldn't blame her.

A short moment after he knocked on the door, he saw the flutter of a curtain at the window, then the rattle of the doorknob.

"Tag!" she exclaimed, as she pulled the door wide. "Is something wrong at the ranch?"

Bemused, he asked, "You think something has to be wrong for me to drop by and say hello?"

She hesitated for only a second. "Well—uh—no. I'm just surprised to see you, that's all. Please come in."

He stepped into the room and waited for her to

deal with the door before he spoke. "I apologize for coming by so late. I did try to call you a couple of times, but the signal on my phone kept failing. I had to bring a mare to Doc's clinic this evening and I just got away from there."

She stood with her hands folded in front of her, surveying him with uncertainty in her eyes. It was obvious she still didn't trust his motives and that frustrated the heck out of him. But maybe she had a right to be suspicious of him, Taggart thought. Especially when he didn't know himself just where his feelings for Emily-Ann were headed.

She said, "You and the Hollisters keep late hours."

"That's part of the job," he said, as he took in the pretty picture she made in a dark red skirt and white blouse. "Were you—er—busy? I don't want to interrupt."

"You're not interrupting. In fact, I was just about to make myself a sandwich. Would you care to join me? Or have you already eaten?"

Relieved that she was inviting him to stay, he took off his hat and raked fingers through his flattened hair. "A sandwich would be great. I haven't eaten since early this morning."

She motioned for him to follow her. "Come with me to the kitchen."

On the way out of the living room, he dropped his hat on an end table, then trailed her through a short hallway that led off in three different directions. A

wide door directly in front of them was open and as
she entered the brightly lit space, he could see it was
an old-fashioned kitchen with knotty pine cabinets
and a single white porcelain sink.

A stack of books was piled at one end of the farm
table and she quickly began moving them to the far
end of the cabinet counter.

"I've been studying for a test. Human anatomy.
The last one I made a B, but I'm afraid this one is
going to be much harder," she said, then gestured for
him to take a seat. "Make yourself comfortable and
I'll get the sandwich makings."

"I can help if you'll tell me what to do," he offered.

"Thanks, but I can manage."

She opened the refrigerator and bent down to the
crisper. Taggart couldn't bring himself to look away
from the rounded shape of her bottom and the way
the fabric of the skirt clung to the tempting curves.

He drew in a deep breath and let it out. "Do you
normally eat this late?"

"No," she answered, with her head still half- hidden in the refrigerator. "After I closed the shop this
afternoon I went out with Camille on a little shopping venture and she insisted we go for milkshakes.
So I'm just now getting a bit hungry."

After piling packages of lunchmeat and cheese
onto the cabinet counter, she glanced over her shoulder at him. "What about you? You didn't have time
to stop for supper?" she asked.

"No. Everyone on the ranch has been very busy. We're getting ready for spring roundup and that takes all hands and the cook."

"Yes, I've heard Camille talk about those days. She and Vivian used to go help." She gathered more items from the refrigerator and shut the door. As she washed a tomato and a head of lettuce at the sink, she said, "I haven't heard from you since we went to Jose's. I'd pretty much decided you probably didn't want to see me anymore."

"Why would I decide that?" he asked, while feeling like a heel. Not that he owed her any explanations. It wasn't like they were a couple or anything. But it was like Blake had implied, Emily-Ann deserved a nice guy. She deserved to be respected and he wasn't giving her that by ignoring her. Nor was he being a nice guy by leading her along to nowhere.

"Personal reasons," she said frankly. "What else?"

Taggart couldn't bear the distance between them. Not while she was talking as though there was nothing between them except a meal and a bit of conversation. Damn it, he'd kissed her. Had she already forgotten that? Or did she have the idea that a kiss meant nothing to him?

How could she possibly figure out what you're thinking? About kissing or anything else, Taggart? She doesn't know who you really are. You haven't told her about Becca or the baby, or any of the things that are still twisting your vision of the future.

Heaving out a heavy breath, he walked over to where she stood. "Well, I could say I've been working overtime and I wouldn't be lying. But that doesn't mean I couldn't have pulled out my phone and sent you a text."

Her gaze locked on the task of slicing the tomato onto a plate, she said, "That notion did cross my mind. But you've mentioned before that you don't like phones. And anyway, it's all okay, Tag. You don't owe me explanations or anything. It's not like we'd planned to see each other again."

Her casual attitude stung him. Which was really stupid. That's the way he wanted things to be with Emily-Ann. Simple and easy with no ties or promises. So why did he want to grab her and hold on? So he could be hurt all over again? And possibly hurt her, too?

Shoving away that dismal thought, he said, "I didn't call or send a message because I've been telling myself that the best thing I could ever do for you is to never see you again. I mean—as in a date."

She dropped the knife and turned to face him. "Why? Because you thought about all those things I told you—about my mother? About the irresponsible bastard who fathered me?"

Frowning, he gently placed his hands on her shoulders. "No! You're not even close. The doubts are inside of me, Emily-Ann. I think you ought to know that when it comes to women—well, several years ago some things happened in my life that changed everything for me. Now, I honestly don't think I could ever be a husband to any woman. And I don't believe I'm supposed to be a father. So you see, if we started dating and getting close…it…wouldn't be fair or right for you."

Her eyes darkened as she continued to stare at him. "Then why did you ask me out in the first place? Why in hell did you kiss me?"

His fingers tightened on her shoulders and it suddenly struck him that trying to be a nice guy was the toughest challenge he'd ever faced. "Because I like you. Because I was lonely and wanted company. Your company. And why do you think I kissed you? You're damned desirable, Emily-Ann. And I'm not made of steel."

"Here's a revelation for you. I'm not made of steel either," she muttered.

Groaning, he said, "Now you're angry with me."

A resigned look came over her face and then she turned away from him and walked to the end of the cabinets. As she pulled out plates and glasses, she said, "No. I'm not angry with you, Tag. In fact, I want to thank you for being honest and not leading me down a dead-end street. That's more than I've ever gotten from other men. It's just that the other night—when we were together—I honestly began to think you might be different. I was wrong. But that's okay, too. I've been a fool before. Many times."

She looked at him and smiled, but the expression didn't reach her eyes. Actually, everything about it said she was looking at the biggest disappointment she'd ever seen in the shape of a man. Until this moment Taggart didn't know it was possible to feel lower than a heel, but he did. He was now on the level of a snake.

"But that doesn't mean we can't still be friends," she told him, then held up a hand as he took a step toward her. "But no kissing. No romance. No ideas that we're going to be a couple. Ever."

He felt sick inside. He felt like he'd been hammered and nailed and tossed aside like a horseshoe that couldn't bend to a shape that would fit.

"That's—uh—fine with me, Emily-Ann. We can be friends and not hurt each other."

"Right. I'm good at being a friend. Not so good at being a lover."

Lover. His lover. Dear Lord, he had to be the biggest hypocrite walking the earth. He was standing here trying to pretend that he wasn't aching to take her to bed right this minute. But having sex with her wouldn't work. No. Not now or ever.

He tried to smile, but the best he could do was twist his lips to a lopsided slant. "Now that we have all that settled, let's have that sandwich. What do you say?"

She didn't smile back at him. Nor did she bother looking him in the eye. Instead, she quickly turned back to the cabinet. "I say the sandwiches are coming right up. And I've changed my mind, you can help by getting ice for the glasses and putting the plates on the table."

Well, that was that, he thought. She knew where he stood and he understood how she felt about it. Problem solved. All he needed to do now was to figure out how to get rid of the empty feeling in the middle of his chest.

With a silent sigh, he rose to his feet and joined her at the cabinet.

It was silly of her to feel deflated, Emily-Ann thought, as she choked down the last bite of ham-and-cheese sandwich. From the very first, she'd known that she didn't have the slightest chance of having any kind of meaningful relationship with Taggart. Even after their evening at Jose's and that kiss on the desert, she'd continually told herself not to set her dreams on the man. She wasn't his kind of woman. And heaven knew he wasn't her kind of man.

And yet, her heart was heavy with disappointment. Maybe if Taggart had been the first man to tell her he wasn't the marrying kind, she could shrug the whole thing off. But now she had to add him to a long list of guys who'd been too commitment shy to give her a serious thought. It was something that had happened to her over and over. And in spite of Camille's optimism that Emily-Ann would find true love someday, she was beginning to accept the fact it wasn't meant for her. Just as it hadn't been meant for her mother.

Rising from her seat at the table, she went over to the cabinet and began filling a coffee maker with grounds and water. "If I'd known you were going to drop by I could've had something better than sandwiches for you. But I do have a few fried apple pies—if you'd like one for dessert."

"No. I've already eaten two sandwiches and most of your potato chips. I don't want to eat up all your groceries," he said.

Shaking her head, she opened a flat plastic container and placed three of the small pies onto a paper plate. "I can't eat them all. Besides, you bought my dinner the other night. So we're even on the groceries. Sort of. You got the short end of the stick."

He smiled at her. "I don't think so."

Grabbing two mugs from the cabinet, she filled them with coffee and carried them and the plate of pies over to the table.

"Did you make these?" he asked as she placed one of the pies onto his plate.

She chuckled. "No. Don't worry. Conchita made these for the shop. Fried pies are something she doesn't do on a daily basis. Just whenever she gets the urge. I'm not that good of a cook. I can do simple things like spaghetti or pork chops and mashed potatoes. I do try brownies once in a while, but they usually turn out like rubber. Conchita tells me I'm cooking them too long. Easy for her to say. She's cooked for fifty years."

"Mmm. The pie is delicious," he said. "And so is the coffee."

She gave him a wry smile. "At least I'm good at that."

He consumed the pie and she motioned for him to take another. "They're small. And I don't want to be tempted. So please eat all of them."

While he continued to eat, she asked, "Was the mare you brought into the clinic injured or something? I hope she's going to be okay."

"She doesn't have any kind of injury. Holt wanted a few tests done on her that Doc could only perform at the clinic. She lost her first foal, so he wants to make sure everything is well with her before he breeds her again."

"It was nice of you to haul her to the clinic for him. I'm sure Holt wants to spend as much time as he can with Isabelle and baby Carter."

Taggart sipped his coffee. "I'm not so sure Holt was going straight home. He wanted to use the extra time to have a talk with Blake. I think the brothers are trying to figure out the situation with Gil and their mother."

Emily-Ann shrugged. "What's to figure out? Gil has moved back and he wants to spend time with Maureen. That's the way I see it."

"Yes, but he's moved into the ranch house with the rest of the family."

"Makes sense to me, too," Emily-Ann said. "The house is huge. Even with Blake and Chandler living there with their families, there's still plenty of room."

Nodding, he said, "On the surface it should be that simple. The way I see it, if Maureen wants to be close to her late husband's brother, then that's her business. Not Blake's or Holt's or anyone else's. But from what Doc has conveyed to me, the brothers are still trying to solve the mystery of Joel's death."

"Don't you mean murder?" she asked grimly, then shook her head. "I realize the family doesn't come out and say those words in front of just any and everybody. But Camille and I have discussed it. And Isabelle has also talked to me about the situation. She says Holt is haunted over the circumstances of his father's death. Camille says the same thing about Matthew."

Nodding soberly, he said, "Losing a loved one is bad all around. But I figure the not knowing makes it even harder for the Hollisters, Gil included. After all, the man lost his brother. Being a detective for thirty years makes Blake and his brothers wonder if he's really come back to Three Rivers to do some investigating of his own, or if he's only interested in their mother."

"Maybe he's interested in both," Emily-Ann reasoned. "I didn't talk to the man that much the night of the party, but he seems very sincere. I only wish—"

He arched an inquisitive brow at her. "What do you wish?"

She looked away from him and sighed. "Only that my mother could've had a man like him in her life."

"Did your mother ever marry?" he asked.

Glancing back at him, she nodded. "Yes, once. Gorman Smith was a salesman from California. Somehow he ended up here in Wickenburg—that was about the time I turned a year old. Back then I think he sold tires or cars. Later on, he turned to selling insurance policies. But never had much money to show for it."

"Where is he now?"

"I have no idea and I'll be happy to keep it that way. As a stepfather, he wasn't abusive or anything. He was just mostly absent, if you know what I mean. The neighbor next door was more of a father to me than Gorman ever was." She clutched her coffee cup and tried to keep her emotions in check. "Iris thought he could do no wrong and when he talked about all of his big dreams, she honestly believed he was going to achieve them. She was always telling me that someday Gorman was going to make our lives much better."

"Did your mother love the man?"

Emily-Ann stared into her coffee cup. "That's

the saddest part about it. She loved him with all her heart."

"I don't see that as sad, Emily-Ann. Loving the man must have made her happy, otherwise she would've kicked him out."

Lifting her gaze to his, she said, "Mom didn't know any better. She was gullible and softhearted and Gorman used that to his advantage. A week hadn't passed after her death when he packed up and lit out."

His eyes narrowed as he studied her face. "Were you grown then?"

"I was eighteen and had just graduated high school. So I suppose I qualified as an adult. I tell you one thing, I was better off with him gone than I would've been with him sitting around drinking beer and bragging about his next moneymaking scheme."

"I'm sorry, Emily-Ann," he said quietly. "I wish it had been different for you and your mother. But you're still very young. You can make your life what you want it to be."

No, Emily-Ann thought. It was impossible to make a man love her if he didn't want to. But then that kind of self-pitying attitude was not going to get her anywhere. In fact, she needed to be smart enough to see that she didn't need a man in her life to make her happy. She didn't need babies like the Hollister families were having right and left. After all, she was going to be a nurse. The profession would provide all the caring and nurturing she needed to feel fulfilled.

"You're so right. And I want to be a nurse. Anything else, I'll leave up to fate."

Rising from her seat, she began to clear the remains of their light supper from the tabletop.

Taggart rose, too, and carried his empty plate and cup over to the sink. "Fate isn't always kind, Emily-Ann."

"Neither are some people."

"I suppose you're talking about me now," he said.

She twisted open the hot water knob and dropped the stopper into the sink. As it filled, she glanced over to see a frown on his face. Both his expression and remark surprised her.

"Why no. I don't think you're unkind at all, Tag."

"Well, I feel very unkind and very phony." His frown was more like a look of anguish as he stepped toward her. "I'm a hypocrite, a liar and a coward to boot. A while ago when I told you I didn't want us to be anything more than friends I was lying. Hell, even as I was speaking the words, I wanted to make love to you."

Make love or have sex. She didn't know which one he meant and her mind was spinning at such a rapid speed she couldn't begin to absorb everything he'd just said. But she had managed to latch on to one key word. *Want*. He wanted her.

"If that's the way you honestly feel, then why did you lie to me?"

Groaning, he wrapped his hands over her shoulders. "I was trying to be a gentleman and do the right thing. Blake says you deserve a nice guy and he's right. You deserve a good man and everything he can give you. But I—" He paused and shook his head with defeat. "These past few minutes I've come to realize that I'm too selfish to give you up to some other man. I want to be the guy who holds you, kisses you—makes love to you."

By the time the last of his huskily spoken words had passed his lips, he was drawing her into the tight circle of his arms and Emily-Ann's heart began to thump so hard and fast she felt light-headed.

Her breathing turned to shallow sips as she dared to flatten her hands against his chest and slide them slowly and surely up to his shoulders. "I lied, too, Taggart. I don't want to be just your friend. I want to be everything to you."

Desire flashed in his brown eyes before his head dropped and his face hovered so close to hers that she could see the pores in his skin, the tiny lines marking his lips.

"Everything," he murmured. "Yes. That's what I want, too."

His soft breath caressed her cheeks and lips and she closed her eyes against the onslaught of sensations rippling over her skin.

She whispered his name but that was all she could manage to say before his lips settled perfectly over hers.

The contact was instant combustion and as his mouth created a firestorm upon her lips, flames spread throughout her body, scorching every spot, every cell it touched.

Beyond the incredible heat washing through her, she was aware of the hard band of his arms tightening around her, drawing her ever closer to the hard wall of his body. Yet it was his kiss that continued to monopolize her senses.

She wanted more. And as his tongue prodded at the opening between her teeth, she realized he felt the same. She opened her mouth to welcome him inside and he immediately began a slow search of the ribbed roof and sharp edges of her teeth. The erotic exploration was more than enough to set off an ache deep between her thighs and, with a needy groan, she wrapped her arms around him and allowed herself to become lost in the total domination of his kiss.

Somehow, her swirling senses managed to register the loud thump of her heartbeat, the humming of the refrigerator and the faint tick of the clock hanging on the wall near the table. Outside the window, the branches of an ash tree scraped against the glass. Strange that she could be aware of all these things and yet not know how much time had marched by since he'd taken her into his arms.

She didn't have a clue as to whether the embrace had gone on for short seconds or several long minutes. Nor did she recognize how the kiss had grown into something far deeper, until his hands latched on to the sides of her hips and pulled them tightly against his. The bulge of his erection straining against his jeans was evidence that he wanted her as much as she wanted him.

She was wrapping her arms around his neck and trying to press herself even closer when he suddenly tore his mouth from hers and stepped back. The unexpected break was so abrupt, Emily-Ann very nearly staggered backward and into the wall of cabinets.

Darting a confused glance at him, she could see he was breathing hard and staring at her with dark, narrowed eyes.

"Tag, what's wrong?" Fearing he was about to bolt from the kitchen, she latched a hand over his forearm. "If you try to tell me that you don't want me, I'll know you're lying. Because you do. Just as much as I want you."

A look of torment came over his face and then he rested his forehead against hers. Emily-Ann couldn't resist slipping her arms around his waist.

"I'm sorry, Emily-Ann. I realize I probably look like an ass to you—or something far worse. But this isn't how I want things for us. I want our time together to be right—special. Not acted out on a hurried whim."

Our time together. The words rolled around in her head, but she dared not take them to heart.

"And how are you going to feel tomorrow, or the next day?" she asked. "Are you going to change your mind again about me—us?"

As she waited for him to answer, she could only think how she didn't want to let him go. She wanted to lead him to her bedroom, shut the door and not let him out until the morning sun was shining through the window.

A wry smile touched his lips. "It wouldn't make any difference if I did. I can't stay away from you. Tonight proves it."

God only knew how very much she wanted to believe him, but so far he'd not done much to help her build any kind of trust.

The doubts circling her thoughts must have shown on her face because he frowned and shook his head.

"You don't believe me," he said.

A sudden feeling of hopelessness washed over her and it cooled the last remnants of the hot desire she'd felt only moments ago. "It's hard to trust you, Tag, when one minute you're hot and the next you're cold. You tell me you want to stay away from me and then you tell me you lied."

She slowly turned away from him and walked over to the table where the last of the leftovers of their meal remained. As she plucked up the bread and a basket of potato chips, he came up behind her and slipped his arms around her waist. His warm body lightly touched hers and she did her best to keep the traitorous stirring in her body far away from the region of her heart.

"Emily-Ann, I don't want to be like the other men who've let you down. I'm trying to be honest," he said, his voice muffled by her hair. "But we've not known each other all that long and it would be wrong of me to start making promises that I can't keep."

Some things happened in my life that changed everything for me.

What could have happened? If it was affecting him that much, why didn't he want to share it with her? She wanted to question him, to demand that he explain. But something told her that now was the wrong time to try to peel away the curtain where he'd hidden his past. Besides, if he ever did truly start to care for her, she wouldn't have to push him to share those things inside him. He'd tell her all on his own.

I know it will happen for you if you just let it.

Camille's advice joined Emily-Ann's tumbling thoughts and suddenly she realized what her dear friend had been trying to tell her. If she ever expected to find love, she was going to have to open her heart and take a chance.

Smiling softly, she turned and looked up at him. "I understand, Tag. Really."

Surprise widened his eyes. "You do?"

Nodding, she reached up and smoothed a finger over the day-old whiskers on his face. "I do. Because I—I'm a little mixed-up. Part of me wants you with a vengeance, while the other part wants to run until I put miles and miles between us."

His sigh was a sound of relief. "That sort of describes what's been going on with me." His hands wrapped gently over her shoulders. "We can figure this out, Emily-Ann. We just need time—together."

"I like the sound of that," she told him.

He bent his head and placed a soft, swift kiss on her lips. "It's not polite to eat and run. But it's getting late and I have a long drive back to Three Rivers." Lifting a hand, he traced fingertips along her cheekbone. "And if I continue to stay I might not be able to leave."

With a clever smile, she looped her arm through his. "And I might not let you leave. So I'll walk you to the door."

Out in the living room, he let himself out and Emily-Ann stood in the open doorway and watched as he crossed the small porch.

When he reached the bottom of the steps, he turned and lifted a hand in farewell. "I'll call you soon," he promised.

She laughed softly. "This from a man who dislikes phones?"

"If it gives me a chance to hear your voice I can

deal with it for a few minutes." He shot her a smile, then disappeared into the shadows shrouding the driveway. After a moment, his truck fired to life and then he was driving away.

Emily-Ann watched until she could no longer see his taillights in the distance, then walked thoughtfully through the house until she reached the kitchen. And as she finished cleaning up the remnants of their meal, she prayed that Taggart wasn't going to make a mess of her heart.

Chapter Seven

With his back propped against a desert willow, Taggart stared into the low flames of the campfire and listened to the distant sound of a ranch hand singing along to the rhythmic twangs of a guitar. The last calf had been turned loose at the branding fire two hours ago. The horses had been fed, watered and confined in a simple rope corral the cowboys had erected next to the wall of a rock bluff. The long day's work had finally ended.

The cowboy's song trailed away, but plenty of sounds remained to fill the silence of the night. A hoot owl joined the crackle of the flames, while in the far distance coyotes yipped and howled.

I've heard that coyotes mate for life.

Even when Emily-Ann had been talking about the wild animals, he'd caught a dreamy, romantic note in her voice. She wanted to think and believe that there was such a thing as true love that lasted forever. But he figured her past held her back from truly believing she'd ever be a part of such a union. Just like his past was throwing up a thick wall every time he tried to picture a long-term future with her.

There were some people that weren't ever meant to live a happily-ever-after, he decided, as he closed his eyes and rubbed fingertips against the weary lids. He didn't know if Emily-Ann was one of those misfortunate few, but he definitely figured he was. Why else would Becca and the baby have been taken away from him so cruelly and suddenly?

He'd been sitting there for several long minutes, his thoughts drifting, when a familiar voice sounded nearby.

"Tag, are you asleep?"

Roused by the question, Taggart opened his eyes to see Chandler standing a few feet away. Since the veterinarian hadn't worked roundup today, he was surprised that the man had driven several miles from the ranch house to join them here at camp tonight.

"I wasn't asleep. Just resting my eyes. I think the hot sun has burned holes in both of them." Taggart slowly pushed himself away from the tree. "What are you doing here? Blake told me you had a heavy day scheduled at the clinic."

"I had a hell of a whopper day at the clinic," he told him. "But it all went well. I came out tonight because Holt and Blake wanted to talk. While Mom isn't here," he added pointedly.

Since they'd started the roundup five days ago, this was the first and only night that Maureen hadn't remained in camp. This evening a couple of hours before dark, she'd ridden back to the ranch to deal with some paperwork that Flo couldn't put off any longer.

"Is anything wrong?" Taggart asked.

Chandler grimaced. "Nothing is wrong. We just rather her not know that her sons are putting their heads together—behind her back, that is."

"I'm sorry. I don't understand. I thought Maureen knew everything about the ranch."

"She does. But this isn't about the ranch. It's about Dad."

"Oh." Taggart reached for his hat lying near his thigh and levered it back onto his head. As he rose from his seat on the ground, he asked, "Is there something you need for me to do?"

"Yes, there is. We want you to join us. We all figure that you're a part of this family now and it wouldn't be good if you didn't know and understand what's going on."

Glancing around, Taggart noticed that sometime

during his drowsy musings, the last of the men had slipped away from the fire to hit their waiting bedrolls.

"Damn, Doc, I'm just the foreman. I don't have any right to sit in on a family meeting."

Chandler frowned at him. "If you had known Dad you would've loved him and he would've felt the same about you. And don't ever let any of us hear you say you're *just* the foreman. That's not the way we are here on Three Rivers. We're family."

Seeing that Chandler was completely sincere, Taggart felt humbled. "All right. Since you put it that way, I'd be honored to sit in."

At the opposite end of the night camp, a chuck wagon and a large tent sat near a huge mesquite tree. A paint horse was tied to a nearby picket line and Taggart recognized it as the late Joel Hollister's personal horse. The one he'd been on when he'd met his death.

"That's Major Bob. How did he get here?" Taggart questioned him about the horse, while thinking Chandler had surely driven one of the four-wheel drive vehicles from the ranch yard.

"I rode him over. Major Bob loves spring roundup and since he's getting a bit of age on him, we don't want to use him hard every day. I'm going to leave him for Mom to ride tomorrow and I'll ride one of the extra mounts back to the ranch tonight. That will make her and Major Bob happy."

And one of the first things Taggart had learned since he'd arrived at Three Rivers Ranch was that one of the main priorities of the Hollister brothers was making their mother happy.

Chandler motioned for Taggart to follow him into the tent and once they were inside, he saw that Blake, Holt and Joseph were sitting in folding chairs along the east wall of the tent, while opposite from them, Gil had taken a seat on the edge of a sleeping cot.

"You guys look like you're getting ready for a poker game where gambling isn't allowed," Chandler attempted to joke as he handed Taggart a folding chair.

"I wish," Joseph said with a grunt, then glanced at Taggart. "Welcome, Tag, glad you're here."

While Taggart gave the youngest Hollister a grateful nod, Chandler said, "None of you need bother telling Tag to keep his mouth shut about this. He already understands Mom isn't to know."

"Good," Holt said, then shot a meaningful glance at his uncle. "Then we all agree that what's said here stays among us?"

The older man leaned forward and rested his elbows on his knees. Just from looking at him, Taggart doubted any man in this tent would want to tangle with him physically, or for that matter, try to match wits with the man. He had a tough, sharp image that reminded Taggart of a drill sergeant he used to know back in Texas.

"Maureen isn't going to hear anything from me that might cause her sadness or worry," Gil said. "You men can rest assured of that."

Holt nodded, then gestured to Joseph. "You're the head investigator, Joe, so you need to be the one to do the talking."

"Don't you think you should key Tag in on the main points?" Chandler spoke up. "He's walked into the middle of this thing without knowing much."

"Right," Joseph said, then glanced at Blake. "You fill him in on what we know and I'll get the evidence."

As soon as the word was spoken, Taggart saw Gil's brows shoot up with sudden interest, but he didn't interrupt with questions. Instead he waited patiently while Blake recounted all they knew about their father's death. Including the horrific way they'd found him hanging from the stirrup of the saddle.

Once Blake finished, Holt said, "You see, Tag, ever since Dad died, we brothers have searched and dug to find the truth of what happened. At first Mother was all for it. And then all of a sudden, she made a complete turn around and ordered us to leave it alone. She didn't want to hear about it or think about it. Basically, she wanted to put the tragedy behind her."

"She has her reasons for that," Gil spoke up.

All five men turned stunned looks on the retired detective.

Blake was the first to speak. "You know what those reasons are?"

"I do," Gil answered. "But I want to see this evidence you have before I say anything."

Taggart got the impression that Holt wanted to press the man for answers, but then he shrugged and said, "Show him, Joe."

The deputy reached behind his chair and retrieved a small cedar box. The sort that women used to store jewelry or other personal trinkets.

"It's not much, Uncle Gil. But it's more than nothing. We've all been thinking that since you've come home to Three Rivers, you'd be willing to help us find Dad's killer. You do think Dad was murdered, don't you?"

Grim-faced, the man said, "I've never thought anything else. None of it made sense. He was too good of a horseman to lose his seat in the saddle. And there was no sensible explanation as to why he rode off by himself that day. The ranch was extremely busy and the way I remember it, he was scheduled to meet with a cattle buyer that afternoon."

"That's right," Joseph agreed, then opened the box and handed it to Gil. "We found the spur rowel first. We know it belonged on Dad's spurs because it's unique and very expensive. Mom gave them to him as a special gift."

Gil placed the rusty rowel in the palm of his hand and studied it as though the piece of metal could give him the answers they all needed. After a moment he returned the rowel to the box and pulled out two tiny pieces of tattered fabric. Taggart could see that it had once been blue plaid, but sun and outdoor elements had faded it.

"That was the shirt Dad was wearing that day," Chandler said, his voice hoarse with emotion.

Joseph explained they'd found the items in two different arroyos on the far side of the ranch property, not far from water well pump number nine.

"But that's not all," Holt said, then turned a questioning look on Joseph. "I thought we agreed we were going to show him the rest?"

"We are," Blake muttered.

"Yeah, the rest." Grim-faced, Joseph fished a piece of paper from his shirt pocket. "I found this not long ago when I was going through Ray's private notes about Dad's case."

"Ray?" Gil questioned. "You mean the late Sheriff Maddox?"

Joseph nodded and Taggart quickly tried to remember where he'd heard that name. But before it could come to his mind, Blake provided the answer.

"In case you don't know, Tag, Ray Maddox was also an old family friend of ours, who happened to be the sheriff of Yavapai County for many years. He was also Tessa's father."

Taggart looked at Joseph, who was holding on

to the square of paper as though it was a snake that could strike any moment.

"So your father-in-law was the late Sheriff Maddox," Taggart said thoughtfully. "Did he inspire you to become a lawman?"

"Partly. He and Uncle Gil inspired me. And I actually worked under Ray for a short time before he became so sick he had to retire. He eventually passed away from a lung disease. That was before Tessa and I married. And before anyone knew he was actually Tessa's father. But that's a long story in itself."

"Yeah," Holt interjected. "Long and twisted. And we don't want to be here all night."

Joseph glanced once again at Taggart. "You can hear the sheriff's story later. But to explain this—" He tapped a finger against the paper in his hand. "Tessa and I live on the Bar X. The ranch was an inheritance from her father and we live in the same house where he always lived. Over time we've discovered lots of notes and papers he left behind. Many of them about Dad's case."

"And this one?" Gil asked. "I'm assuming it has some sort of clue."

Joseph said, "Ray seemed to think it important enough to put in his files. But it was something he never shared with our family before he died. We've concluded that he probably kept it to himself for Mother's sake. And we sure as hell don't want her finding out about it. Not unless it proves pertinent.

If that's the case, we won't have a choice. We'll have to tell her and our sisters."

He handed the paper to Gil and as the man quickly scanned the notes, Taggart noticed all four of the Hollister brothers were watching intently for his reaction.

Finally Gil looked up and Taggart could see something like wry acceptance on his face.

"This is—" He muttered a curse, then let out a chuckle that wasn't anything close to an expression of humor. "It's obviously going to come as a surprise to you guys, but Maureen already knows about the woman at the stockyards in Phoenix. She talked to me about it months ago."

Stunned silence followed the man's revelation and Taggart watched the four brothers exchange bewildered glances.

Blake was the first to speak. "Mother knows? How? None of us have breathed a word about it."

Gil said, "She was going through some of Joel's old business correspondence and happened to run into a small day planner with notes about meetings he had scheduled. Several entries were things like— see her during the sale. And—she'll be waiting outside. From the dates posted next to the notes, they're close to the time that Joel died."

Incredulous, all four brothers stared at him as they tried to digest this news.

Eventually, Blake said, "She hasn't said a word to us about it. Why?"

"Yeah, why?" Holt demanded. "Why did she tell you and not us?"

Instead of taking offense at Holt's accusing tone, Gil shook his head and quietly explained, "She didn't want any of her children to get the idea that their father might've been an adulterer. That's why she's been so preoccupied for the past months. She's been worried you guys might uncover the fact that Joel had been associating with a woman before he died. That's why she kept ordering you all to leave the whole matter alone."

"Oh my God," Joseph murmured.

Chandler looked sick as he pulled off his hat and raked a hand through his hair. "We've been stupid," he said flatly. "Mother is stronger than all of us put together. We should've known she could handle whatever we uncover. Now all this worrying and sneaking about has been wasted time."

"That's hardly the point now," Blake said, then leveled his attention on Gil. "The crux of the matter is does *she* think Dad was an adulterer? Furthermore, do you?"

Gil grimaced. "Do you really have to ask that question, Blake? Neither one of us could ever believe such a thing about Joel. Maureen was everything to him. No. There had to be some other reason for him to be associating with a woman."

His expression calculating, Joseph nodded in agreement. "I have a feeling this woman, whoever she was, might be the key to the whole mystery."

"Exactly, Joe," Gil said. "We need to try to identify and locate her."

"Does that mean you're going to help us?" Holt asked his uncle. "Joe's a damned good deputy, but I figure all of our heads put together is better than one."

Joseph shot Holt an appreciative grin. "Thanks, Holt, for the compliment. But you're right. We need to work together on this."

With that decided, the men began to offer suggestions on how to go about identifying the mystery woman. Taggart was content to sit back and take it all in. But as soon as there was a lull in the conversation he decided to speak up.

"I'm just a listener here," Taggart said. "But I do have a question. Are you going to let your sisters in on this information? And are you going to tell your mother that you guys have been aware of *the woman* for the past few months?"

"Those are good questions, Tag," Blake said, then looked to his brothers for answers. "What about it, guys? Should we tell our sisters?"

Joe was the first to answer. "I vote no. Not until we figure out whether any of this information is relevant."

"I agree," Chandler said. "Camille is pregnant

and running her diner. She doesn't need the extra worry. And Vivian already has enough stress with baby twins and a teenager, plus her job as a ranger. And we know how both of them adored Dad. They considered him a saint."

"He wasn't a saint, but close to it," Gil said. "And I think all of you are not giving your sisters enough credit. They would never consider the idea that Joel had a mistress or anything close to it."

"Probably not," Holt agreed. "But the whole issue about *the woman* would worry them. Just like it nags at us guys. Who was she? And why was Dad seeing her? I vote no. If we learn more, then we can let Viv and Camille in on it."

"I vote no, also," Blake said firmly, then glanced at his uncle. "What about Mother, do we tell her?"

"I think it might save some awkward feelings if I explain the situation to her," Gil said. "She thinks she's protecting all of you by trying to sweep the issue under the rug. She needs to understand that finding the truth will be better for the whole family."

Taggart wholly agreed with the man. Nothing good could ever come from hiding things. Ever since he'd left Emily-Ann's house, five nights ago, he'd begun to realize that more and more.

Until he explained about Becca and the baby, Emily-Ann would never be able to understand his reluctance to get involved in a serious relationship. If he ever expected to have a life that included her, he would have to find the courage to confess what losing them had done to him. Yet the scarred part of his heart kept asking why bother to pour out all those bad memories. Doing such a thing wouldn't take away his fear of loving and losing a second time.

Love. He'd seen the emotion here tonight with the Hollister men. Love was guiding the decisions they made concerning their family. Love caused them to put the feelings of others first, rather than their own. And as Taggart had listened to them, he'd begun to wonder if he'd ever truly loved anyone.

He'd believed Becca was his true love and when she'd told him that she was pregnant, he'd wanted the child just as much as he'd wanted her. At that time, he'd been twenty-two and considered himself old enough and man enough to deal with the responsibility of a family. But now as he looked back on their brief marriage, he wondered if he'd been more infatuated with the idea of proving to himself he was a better man than his father, rather than truly loving Becca.

So what were these feelings that were pushing him toward Emily-Ann? he wondered. He'd been trying to convince himself they were nothing but lust. He'd not made love to a woman in a long time. So long that he didn't even want to think about it. And yet, something told him that going to bed with Emily-Ann wasn't going to satisfy the hunger she'd built in him.

"Want to go have a cup of coffee, Tag? I think the pot is still hanging over the campfire."

Chandler's voice pulled Taggart out of his deep musings and he looked up to see Chandler standing in front of him. Directly behind him, the other men were filing out of the open flap of the tent.

Quickly rising from the chair, he said, "Sorry. I—was doing some thinking. I didn't realize the meeting had ended. I think I need that coffee in the worst kind of way."

Smiling, Chandler gave his shoulder a friendly pat. "I'm the one who should be apologizing. You just got started as foreman and you've had to jump straight into spring roundup. You have a lot on your mind and I've made matters worse by dragging you into this family issue about Dad."

"No. Don't apologize," Taggart told him. "I'm glad I was here and glad that I know what's going on with your father's investigation. I just wish I could help in some way. If Joe ever wants me to ride with him to look for more evidence, I'd be happy to."

"I'm sure he'll take you up on the offer," Chandler told him. "Now let's go have the last of the coffee before it turns to black mud."

Emily-Ann laughed as she watched the baby boy cuddled in Isabelle's arms take a tiny taste of sugary frosting from his mother's finger.

"Look at that puckered expression on his face," Emily-Ann exclaimed. "He thinks it's awful."

Laughing with her, Isabelle glanced down at her son. "Just give him a year or two and then he'll change his mind about the taste of sugar—unfortunately. I never knew a man who didn't have a sweet tooth. I'm sure little Carter will have one, too."

The two women and baby were sitting outside the coffee shop at one of the wrought iron tables. Late afternoon sun was flickering through the limbs of the mesquite tree, while a breeze helped to cool the flimsy shade. When Isabelle and the baby had shown up, Emily-Ann had been on the verge of closing shop, but she'd gladly put the task on pause in order to visit with her friend.

"I'm so glad you had a chance to come by," Emily-Ann told her.

Isabelle offered the baby his pacifier. "I know I'm keeping you from closing up, but I wanted to stop and chat with you for a few minutes."

"I'm glad you did. I rarely get to see you and Carter. He's growing so fast. And he looks just like Holt. But I'm sure you hear that all the time."

The pretty blonde grinned as she shifted the baby's weight against her arm. "All the time. But that's okay. His daddy is a handsome devil."

Both women laughed at that and then Emily-Ann sighed as she continued to study the baby's sweet face. "Gosh, it doesn't seem like it's been that long ago when you first met Holt. You came by here hopping mad because he wouldn't give you the time of day."

Chuckling, Isabelle rolled her eyes. "You kept telling me Holt was a dreamy hunk. I thought you were crazy. He was so infuriating I wanted to slap his face."

"Now look. You two are happily married and you have little Carter Edmond."

"I have to admit you were right, Emily-Ann. Holt has made me so happy."

Emily-Ann smiled gently at her friend. "You know, you're the first and only woman who's ever asked me to be their maid of honor. You can't imagine how special that made me feel."

Isabelle reached across the table and squeezed Emily-Ann's hand. "I moved here to Arizona not knowing a single soul and you were so kind to me. You were the first person to befriend me and I'll never forget that."

Emily-Ann waved a dismissive hand through the air. "Being your friend was and is my pleasure."

After a long sip of iced coffee, Isabelle asked, "Have you seen Camille lately?"

"Last week. With roundup going on, I think she was going to drive up to the reservation and spend a day with Vivian and the kids. Otherwise, I guess she's been hanging close to Three Rivers. Normally she would go out to camp and stay the night, but with the baby coming she says she needs a soft bed to sleep in."

"Amen to that," Isabelle agreed, then added, "Actually, Holt texted me earlier in the day and said that roundup was wrapping up and that everyone would be heading back to the ranch this evening. So our men will finally be home."

That meant Taggart would be home, too. Since roundup started six days ago, he'd actually sent her three text messages. All had been short and simple. More or less to let her know things were going well and that he was thinking of her. But did that mean he would be anxious to see her again? Several days had passed since he'd stopped by her house and they'd wound up having that heated kiss in the kitchen. Considering the fickle way his mind worked, she could only guess how Taggart might be feeling about her now.

Isabelle's expression took a shrewd turn. "I heard in a roundabout way that Tag took you out to dinner. How did that go?"

Emily-Ann felt her cheeks turn a hot pink. "How did you hear that? I haven't told anyone about our date. Not even Camille."

"Blake mentioned it to Holt. I think they were surprised, because the foreman is such a quiet kind of guy when he's around them. He never talks about going out or doing much socially. But you know how the old saying goes. It's those quiet ones that are real tigers underneath."

Emily-Ann was suddenly remembering their heated embrace. At that moment she wouldn't have hesitated to make love to him. And since then, she'd thought of little else. "I don't think he's actually the dating sort. He more or less told me that he asked me out because he was lonely."

"Aww. That's awful. Uh—not that he asked you for a date, but that he was lonely. It's terrible to feel that way. I remember how it felt after my divorce and I moved here to Yavapai County. I lived out there on Blue Stallion Ranch all alone, with no one to talk to but the horses and the wind. And then Ollie and Sol came. Those two old men were a lifesaver."

Not wanting to dwell on the idea of Taggart being lonely, Emily-Ann changed the subject. "How are Ollie and Sol, by the way? Remind me before you leave and I'll sack up some leftover pastries for them."

"Thanks. Both men are doing great. They'll love getting the pastries."

"And your mother? She didn't want to come to town with you today?"

Isabelle let out a wry laugh. "Are you joking? And be away from Sam for that long? Mom met him over at the Bar X early this morning and they've been out riding horses all day. She's going to be too stiff to walk tomorrow."

"So are they planning a wedding yet?"

The baby began to squirm and fuss. Isabelle placed him against her shoulder and gently patted his back. "Oh yes. At first they insisted they both wanted a quiet simple ceremony. But I think they're realizing that won't work. How do you do quiet and simple with all the Hollister family and Sam's countless friends? Not to mention Mother's long-time friends from San Diego. I told her they should elope to Vegas. Sam loves whiskey and cards. He ought to enjoy it."

Emily-Ann was laughing in agreement when she heard the cell phone in the pocket of her skirt announce an incoming message.

"Excuse me, Isabelle. I'd better check this," she said as she retrieved the phone. "I'm expecting to hear from Conchita. She wasn't feeling well this morning and I've been half-afraid she's going to have to miss cooking pastries for tomorrow."

Emily-Ann quickly opened her message box and then promptly felt her jaw drop.

Isabelle quickly questioned, "What is it? Is something wrong?"

"No. Uh—it's not Conchita. The message is from Tag. He wants to know if I want to come over for supper. He'll cook for me."

A wicked twinkle appeared in Isabelle's brown eyes. "That's a long drive out to Tag's place. Do you think it would be worth it?"

Emily-Ann's short laugh sounded like a breathless schoolgirl and she realized she was reacting idiotically. "Well—yes. But I—" Pausing, she released a long sigh. "To be honest, Isabelle, I don't know if seeing Tag will end up meaning anything."

Frowning, Isabelle asked, "Why? The whole Hollister family has been raving about him. He must be a good man. And if he's interested in you—that's a beginning. Or maybe you're not attracted to the man."

Emily-Ann groaned. "I might get a little daffy at times, but I'm not completely crazy. Have you looked at him?" she asked, then shook her head. "No. Probably not. Because the only man you see is Holt. But Tag is—a hot hunk. How do you think I could not be attracted to him?"

"By the hesitant tone I hear in your voice," Isabelle reasoned. "Something about the man worries you."

Biting down on her bottom lip, Emily-Ann turned her gaze to the nearby street. "I'm afraid he's going to end up being like all the rest, Isabelle. The kind that just can't do commitment."

Isabelle snorted. "Don't you think it's a bit too early to be pinning that sort of label on the man? Just think about all the concerns I had about Holt. Everyone in Yavapai County knew he was a womanizer—even me. But I took a chance that he could change and would change. It takes some courage, Emily-Ann, but you might find that Tag just might be worth the risk."

She thoughtfully studied her friend. "I can't imagine how brave you had to be to marry Holt Hollister."

Her smile full of love, Isabelle turned her head and pressed a soft kiss to baby Carter's cheek. "Right. And who knows, someday Tag might give you a little guy like this."

A baby? It wasn't difficult to see herself making love to Taggart. But after that, everything about her future went gray. The only thing she could see was how her mother must have felt when she'd been abandoned by her lover, and her family, because she was pregnant. It wasn't that Emily-Ann would ever be afraid to raise a child on her own. Anything her mother could do, she was positive she could do. But no way did she want a child to ever feel as shunned by its father as Emily-Ann had felt all these years.

"You're just like Camille," Emily-Ann said teasingly, "always trying to find me a husband."

"Well, you did catch Camille's bridal bouquet. That's definitely a sign of things to come."

Emily-Ann let out a loud groan. "Oh, not you, too."

Isabelle looked confused. "What's wrong? What did I say?"

"Nothing. I'll just say that the next time I touch a bridal bouquet, it'll have to be my own. Otherwise, I'm not going near it!"

A comical look on her face, Isabelle said, "Okay, if you say so. Right now I've got to get home. I've been training three young colts and two fillies. And I've not yet ridden the girls today. I need to get home and do that before daylight goes and Holt gets home."

Holding the baby in one arm, Isabelle started to gather up the trash on the table with her free hand, but Emily-Ann quickly brushed her aside.

"Forget that," she told her. "I'll clean up here."

"Thanks."

Isabelle shouldered her purse and Emily-Ann plucked up Carter's diaper bag and accompanied her friend to the truck she was driving.

After Isabelle and the baby were safely strapped in for the trip back to Blue Stallion Ranch, she stuck her head out the open window of the vehicle. "Call me in a few days and let know how supper with Tag goes."

Emily-Ann frowned at her. "I didn't say I was going."

Isabelle let out a calculating laugh. "Who are you trying to fool? You and I both know that you're going."

Her friend drove away and without giving it another thought, Emily-Ann pulled the phone from her pocket and tapped out a message to Taggart.

I'll be there by six thirty.

Before she walked back to the table where she

and Isabelle had been sitting, her phone dinged with his reply.

Great. I'll see you then.

Chapter Eight

After six days of riding through thorny chaparral, wrestling calves and spending his nights on the ground in a sleeping bag, Taggart should have felt too tired to do anything except collapse on the bed and stay there. But the idea of seeing Emily-Ann again was enough to energize him.

For the past two hours, he'd been rushing around the house straightening the rooms as best as he could, showering and changing into a respectable pair of jeans and shirt, then cooking what he thought would be a halfway presentable meal for Emily-Ann.

After chopping salad and baking potatoes, he was

about to throw steaks into an iron skillet when he heard her knock on the front door.

Setting the cuts of beef aside, he made his way through the house until he reached the front door. When he swung it wide, she was standing on the edge of the porch, petting one of Chandler's cur dogs.

"I see you've met King," Taggart said, while he took in the sight of her smooth red hair hanging to her waist and the pink-and-white flowered dress clinging to her curves. She looked luscious and as pretty as sunshine on a Sunday morning.

Smiling, she continued to stroke the dog's head. "He's beautiful. Is he yours?"

He stepped out of the doorway and walked over to her. "No. He's one of Doc's many dogs. King likes me, so when I left the ranch yard this evening, he decided to follow. Halfway here, I felt sorry for the guy and stopped and let him ride in the truck the rest of the way."

She straightened away from the dog and Taggart leaned forward to press a kiss on her cheek. Her skin was soft and smelled like a gentle rain on a meadow of wildflowers. It was all he could do not to gather her into his arms and taste her lips.

"Hello," he murmured as he forced his head to lift away from hers.

Her gaze darted shyly up to his and the warmth he saw in the green depths made everything about being with her feel good and right.

"Hello, Tag."

"I'm glad you're here," he said.

The corners of her lips lifted ever so slightly. "I'm glad I'm here, too."

She gestured to the dog. "I take it that Chandler doesn't mind King having a second home."

"Not at all. Doc knows I'll bring him back home in the morning." He pushed the door wide and gestured for her to come in. "After I sent the invitation for supper, I worried you might not want to make the long drive out here at night."

They entered the living room where she paused to take a slow survey of the leather furniture, dark green drapes and a large braided rug. To Taggart the room looked fine, but from a woman's perspective it probably looked stark.

She said, "It doesn't bother me to drive at night. I know the road well and there's hardly ever any traffic out this way. Especially after you turn onto Three Rivers' property."

"Hopefully, you'll think my cooking is worth it," he said with a smile. "But before we head to the kitchen, I should warn you not to expect much. With me being gone on roundup this past week, I've not had time to restock my cupboards."

"I can eat anything. Even soggy oatmeal."

"I promise it won't taste that bad. And I do have a nice surprise." He walked over and took her by the arm. "Come on and I'll show you."

"Your house is nice," she said as he guided her to the kitchen. "I like the arched doorways and the floors are real wood. Did you put the polished gleam on them?"

He laughed. "Are you kidding? If I sweep once a week that would be a miracle. This house isn't large by most standards, but it's the biggest one I've ever lived in. I'm about to decide I'm going to have to hire a cleaning lady to keep it looking livable."

"Hmm. That would be a big help. I suppose Jazelle doesn't have time to do it for you. She's already stretched pretty thin helping Reeva in the kitchen and Roslyn and Katherine with the babies. And then she has Raine, her own little boy to take care of whenever she goes home. He's about five now, I think."

"I saw Raine a few days ago. Nick, Blake's teen-aged son, brought the boy down to the ranch yard to see the cows and horses. He's a cute little fellow. By the way, I've never asked anyone, but does Jazelle have a husband?"

"No. She's never been married." She cast him a sly look. "Jazelle is very pretty—you've obviously noticed."

He slanted her an impish grin. "She's pretty, but she's not you. And I was wondering because of the little boy. That day I saw him at the cattle barn I got the feeling he didn't have a daddy."

"That's very perceptive of you."

He tried not to grimace. "I'm experienced with the subject of missing fathers."

"Well, so am I," she said, then promptly changed the subject. "Now what is this surprise you have?"

They entered the kitchen and he led her over to the cabinet counter where the pie Reeva had given him was wrapped in aluminum foil.

"Bless her sweet heart, Reeva sent word for me to come to the big house—that she had something for me. She got the idea that I deserved a pie for wrapping up my first roundup here on Three Rivers. I told her I was going to share it with you."

"That was thoughtful." She sneaked a peek under the edge of the foil. "Oh, it's pecan!"

"One of my favorites," he said.

She chuckled. "One?"

"I have many."

She looked at him and in that moment, Taggart realized how much he'd missed her these past few days and how very much he wanted her now.

Wrapping his hands around her upper arms, he looked into her eyes and suddenly without warning, a soft, mushy feeling spread throughout his chest.

Damn. What was the matter with him? How could this woman make him feel happy and vulnerable at the same time? It didn't make sense. But he'd heard there was no logic to being in love. Could that be what was happening to him? Whatever the reason for this strange upheaval inside him, he didn't want to think it was love. That was for other people.

"Is something wrong?" she asked. "You're looking at me like I have a smudge on my nose or something."

He released the long breath he hadn't realize he'd been holding until now. "Sorry. I guess I've been staring. It's just that you look so beautiful tonight I—can't help myself."

An impish smile wrinkled her nose. "Are you feeding me cheese as an appetizer?"

"If I am it's not the fake processed kind. It's the real deal."

He tried to smile back at her and lighten the moment, but the emotions swirling through him wouldn't allow him to do anything other than place a kiss on her forehead.

When his lips continued to linger against her skin, both her hands reached out and anchored a hold on the front of his shirt.

"I probably shouldn't be so obvious, but I've missed you, Tag."

His insides began to quiver with longing and he drew in another deep breath and blew it out. "I'd like to kiss you and show you how much I've missed you. But I'm afraid if I did, we might never get to eat."

Laughing softly, she purposely stepped away from him and moved down the cabinets until she reached a large gas range with a built-in grill on top. "You're cooking steaks," she said, observing the two pieces of meat soaking in a bowl of dark-colored marinade.

"I'm guessing you would probably prefer chicken, but steak was the only thing left in the freezer."

"I love steak. But I do have a question. Why cook them in a skillet when you have this great indoor grill that most people would give their eye teeth for?"

Joining her at the stove, he switched on the blaze beneath the black skillet.

"Because the iron gives it a flavor I like," he explained. "But I can grill yours if you'd rather have it cooked that way."

"Oh, no. I'm anxious to taste the difference."

"Coming right up." He tossed a chunk of butter into the skillet and gathered up the bowl containing the cuts of meat.

Next to him, Emily-Ann asked, "Can I do something to help?"

The best thing she could do to help him, Taggart thought, would be to tell him to forget about the supper and make love to her. But his mind was taking rapid leaps into uncertain territory. Emily-Ann might be thinking about food and nothing more.

Jerking his thoughts back to the present, he gestured to a row of cabinets to the right of them. "You might start with setting the table and icing some glasses. Unless you want to drink wine or beer."

As she headed to the cabinets, she said, "I'll skip the spirits tonight. You never know when an antelope or deer might walk onto the road. And I did promise I'd drive carefully for you. Remember?"

Hell yes, he remembered. That night he'd come very, very close to telling her about Becca and the car crash that had taken her and the unborn baby, and ended the future he'd planned for their lives together. But just when he'd thought he could get the painful words out to Emily-Ann, a barrier of some sort had lodged in his throat and he'd done well to breathe, much less talk about the incident that continued to shadow the choices he made for himself.

"I do remember," he murmured. "And I'm glad you're being cautious—for my sake and yours."

More than an hour later, after Emily-Ann and Taggart had finished eating the meal and pieces of Reeva's pecan pie, she insisted on helping him put the kitchen back in neat order.

After the last dish was dried and put away, Taggart said, "There's a bit of coffee left. Might be nice to have a cup out on the front porch. Unless you'd prefer to stay inside."

Throughout the meal, Emily-Ann had tried to keep her gaze from constantly straying to Taggart, but she'd mostly failed at the effort. The days they'd been apart had felt like ages to her and everything about him, from his dark wavy hair, to the warm light in his brown eyes and the stubble on his chin, was mesmerizing her. While they'd worked side by side doing the dishes, her fascination for him had only increased and several times she'd had to catch herself from reaching over and touching him.

Sitting outside in the cool night air might be enough to put a brake on her runaway urges, she thought, but she doubted it.

"The porch sounds great," she agreed.

Taggart poured their coffee and with cups in hand, they walked back through the house and onto the front porch. At one end a wide, wooden swing hung from the rafters, while on the opposite end, a group of wicker furniture with tropical-printed cushions invited a person to relax.

"Where would you like to sit?" he asked.

"The wicker looks comfy, but I love to swing. Is that okay with you?"

"I've spent so many hours in the saddle this past week that a wooden swing will feel like I'm sitting on a cloud," he assured her.

With a hand resting against the small of her back, he guided her over to the swing. King, who'd been lying in the shadows, followed them across the porch and waited until they were seated before he flopped down on the floor near Taggart's feet.

"It's a lovely evening," Emily-Ann remarked.

His arm came around the back of her shoulders and a soft sigh slipped past her lips.

"If it's too cool for you I can go in the house and find a jacket," he offered.

Even if she'd been freezing, she wouldn't have wanted him to move. Snuggled next to his side, with the warmth of his thigh pressed against hers and the low, raspy sound of his voice in her ear, she wondered how something that felt so good could possibly last. It couldn't. Not for her. But she wasn't going to allow herself to worry about that tonight.

"I'm fine," she told him. "Besides, who can pay attention to the chill in the air with a view like this?"

Situated at the foot of a ridge of rocky hills, the house was shrouded by several mesquite trees, but the gnarled limbs didn't block the landscape directly in front of them. Beneath the starlit sky, she could see a shadowy vista of wide-open range peppered with tall century plants, Joshua trees and saguaro cactus. To the right, in the far distance, the lights illuminating the Three Rivers Ranch yard glowed like a beacon in the wilderness.

Normally Emily-Ann would have been hypnotized by the beauty, along with the pleasant sounds of the breeze whispering through the mesquites and the call of the night birds. But all those things were just a lovely backdrop to Taggart's presence.

"Blake told me this house was built back in the late 1950s by his grandfather. Back then, the foreman of Three Rivers had a big family and needed a place to live," Taggart explained. "All I can say is that the Hollisters didn't hold back, this house would've been expensive to build even back then."

While he was talking, his fingers had begun to trace abstract designs against her arm. The light, feathery touch against her skin was creating far more goose bumps than the cool night breeze and it was all she could do to focus on his words.

"When Camille and I were in elementary school, I remember the foreman who lived here was an older man with a wife and five kids. Then about the time we became teenagers, he retired and the family moved away. That's when Matthew took over." She glanced curiously over at him. "Did you have a house of your own when you worked on the Flying W?"

He shook his head. "No. I didn't live directly on the ranch. I had a place of my own not far from the nearest town, which was Canyon. The commute back and forth to the ranch wasn't all that bad. But this—" He paused and gestured to his surroundings. "It's like nothing I've ever dreamed. To be honest, when I sent my résumé to the Hollisters for this job, I didn't think I had a chance in hell of getting it. But I didn't see any harm in trying. Sometimes miracles do happen."

Like her sitting here with a man like him, she thought. She'd never dreamed a man of Taggart's caliber would ever ask her out for dinner, much less cook for her. To be fair, the men she'd dated in her past hadn't been losers. But most of them had still been floundering around, struggling to figure out what they wanted to do with their lives. Some of them hadn't had a clue how to better themselves, while others were working on plans.

Even so, they'd all had one thing in common, having a little fun with her, and then moving on. These past few weeks, she'd been telling herself that Taggart had to be different. He was responsible and settled. He was admired and successful. She just didn't yet know if he'd want to be in her life for the long haul.

She placed her cup on a small table situated close to the arm of the swing, then reached over and covered his hand with hers. "If you hadn't sent in your résumé, I would've probably never met you. Or do you believe in fate and that our paths would've crossed somewhere at some point in our lives?"

The gentle look on his face stirred her heart with feelings so tender they brought a rush of moisture to her eyes. Oh my, what was this man doing to her? She felt like a fallen leaf at the mercy of the desert wind. He was carrying her away, tumbling and swirling, and she could only hope she didn't end up landing at the bottom of a steep arroyo with no way of climbing out.

"I do believe in fate," he answered, his voice pensive. "Sometimes it's good, other times it's bad."

"Yes," she solemnly agreed. "And my mother's fate was mostly bad."

He turned his head and for long moments he studied her face as though he was weighing whether he could trust her. With what, she didn't know.

Finally he said, "You've probably noticed that I don't talk about my mother much. Not because I didn't love her—I loved her very much. But talking about her hurts. A lot. And I'm beginning to think you understand how that feels."

"It's never easy to talk about my mother," she murmured. "And even when I think about her, it puts an ache in my chest. She had a rough life, but I try to put that out of my mind and remember the good times we shared as mother and daughter. That helps."

Nodding, he glanced down at the yellow cur sleeping at his feet. "When I was twenty-three my mother, Carolyn, died of a heart attack. She'd never been in perfect health, but her death was totally out of the blue. Or that's the way it had felt at the time. But after I'd had time to think about everything, I realized it was a miracle she'd lived as long as she did."

This was the first time he'd ever really talked about his family and, as she studied his solemn profile, it was fairly obvious that his young life hadn't been easy. "Your mother had a chronic health problem?"

Her question elicited a cynical snort from him.

"No. Her husband—my father, Buck O'Brien was the chronic problem. To put it plainly, the man was a selfish bully. He did his best to keep her and us kids browbeaten. He made her life pure hell. And me and my sister—we just clung to Mom and tried to stay invisible."

This was the first time she'd ever heard such bitterness in his voice and, though it was an ugly sound, she could understand where it was coming from. She'd had plenty of experience dealing with the negative emotion and knew firsthand that once it took root inside a person, it was hard to push aside.

"Were your parents married when she passed away?" Emily-Ann ventured to ask.

His gaze left King to settle on her face. "Oh, yes. At that time he'd been scrounging around the area between Canyon and Hereford taking on little construction jobs wherever he could find them. He was working as a carpenter during that time, but that was only when he really wanted to work. Mom was the one who paid the bills and kept things afloat for them. Not him. She had a bookkeeping job at the same feeder lot where I worked tending cattle."

Emily-Ann shook her head. "Gorman, my stepfather, was mostly shiftless, too. But in most other ways he was very kind to Mother. So I can sort of understand why she loved him and remained married to him. But if your father was actually mean to your mother, why didn't she divorce him?"

Sighing, he gently trailed his forefinger over the back of her hand and down each of her fingers. "I can't answer that, Emily-Ann. Maybe because the choices she made were something only a woman could understand. Or maybe because I've never been in love like that—where a person is blinded to the other's faults. I often wanted to blame it on the fact that she was insecure. She didn't think she could survive without him. But in truth, she would've made it so much better on her own."

Losing her mother had knocked Emily-Ann flat and it had taken her a long time to pull herself together and move forward. She'd often heard that losing a mother was even harder for a man to deal with. Whether that was true or not, she could tell, just from the pain in his voice, that Taggart had suffered deep grief.

"Your mother didn't want to be on her own, Tag. Just like mine didn't want to be," she reasoned, then asked, "What happened with your father after Carolyn died? You mentioned that you don't see him often, but does he still live in that part of Texas?"

"He comes and goes. My sister and I never really know when he's going to leave or show up. Usually when we see him it's because he wants money."

She stared at him in disbelief. "The man asks his children for money? That would take some gall."

"He's got that in spades," Taggart said, his voice heaped with sarcasm.

She turned her hand over and wrapped her fingers tightly around his. "When I first met you, Tag, I would've never guessed that our lives were similar.

We both lost our mothers and we both suffered be-cause of the choices they made in their lives."

"Yes. But there's more to mine, Emily-Ann. I—uh—"

When he faltered, then failed to say anything more, she prompted, "You what?"

His gaze continued to delve deep into hers until she thought he was going to ignore her question com-pletely. And then a long breath rushed out of him and he said, "I've been married."

Stunned, she stared at him while questions darted wildly through her mind. "Married? I suppose that means you're divorced?"

Pressing the toe of his boot against the floor of the porch, he paused the gentle movement of the swing.

"No," he said. "It means I'm a widower."

Her gasp was so loud that King lifted his head and looked at her.

"A widower," she repeated blankly, then shook her head. "You were married and your wife died?"

"No, she didn't just die. She wrecked the car she was driving and it killed her and our unborn child."

His revelation struck her so hard that her stomach made a sickening roll. "Oh. Oh my, Tag. I—don't know what to say."

"You don't have to say anything," he said wryly. "I just—felt like it was time that I told you about Becca and the baby. I thought that—well, you ought to know why I've been shy about getting involved with you."

Several years ago some things happened in my life that changed everything for me.

The words he'd spoken to her that night when he'd come to her house were suddenly skipping through the forefront of her mind. His comment hadn't made complete sense to her then, but it was becoming clear now.

"I'm so sorry," she murmured. "I thought your reluctance was all about me—not meeting your standards."

"That was stupid thinking on your part, Emily-Ann. You meet all my standards and more. I think that's why—when I look at you—when I'm with you like this, I get so scared I can hardly breathe. I tell myself that I can't take another chance with a woman. But then when I'm away from you, I hurt to be back with you."

Agony was wrapped around his every word. It knotted his voice and twisted his rugged features. She wanted to take it all away. She wanted to slip her arms around him and assure him that tragedy wasn't likely to strike twice. But she couldn't move, or think beyond the notion that he'd been in love with another woman. So much so that he'd married her. That the two of them had been expecting a child together.

"I—how long ago did this happen?" she finally managed to ask.

"Ten years ago. I was twenty-one when I first met Becca and turned twenty-two when we got married. She was two months pregnant when we stood before the county judge and exchanged vows. She didn't want to get married then. She wanted to wait until the baby was born. She didn't want folks thinking I'd married her because I had to."

Emily-Ann couldn't stop herself from asking, "Did you?"

"No. I mean, yes, I did feel obligated when I'd learned she was pregnant, but no one was holding a gun to my back. I believed I loved her."

Emily-Ann's brows lifted as she watched his features twist even tighter. "You believed? You weren't sure?"

He groaned. "Back then I thought I was sure about my feelings for her—about getting married and everything that went with that decision. Looking back on it all, I don't know. We were so young. I did care for her deeply and the baby—I was a little scared at becoming responsible for a child, but I wanted it. Wanted it with all my heart. But four months after we married, they were both gone from my life."

Oh God, Emily-Ann thought sickly. How could she ever expect to compete with the ghost of his wife and unborn child? Ten years had passed and he was still tortured over losing them.

"Four months. You'd hardly begun your married

life together. You must have felt like your whole world was turned upside down."

"To be honest, I was so numb everyone around me was probably thinking I'd turned into a zombie. And then just about the time I was beginning to wake up and start living again, Mom was struck by the heart attack. All of it together just about wiped me out."

The mere thought of the grief he'd gone through squeezed her heart with pain. "I can only imagine," she murmured.

His eyes softened and then his fingers gently smoothed the hair at her temple. "It was a bad, bad time," he admitted. "But now—meeting you has made everything different for me. You're the first woman since Becca that I've ever really wanted—or needed."

Wanted. Needed. But not loved.

Even as the thought zipped through her brain, she realized it was wrong of her to think it. She and Taggart hadn't known each other that long. She couldn't expect him to fall instantly in love with her. Actually, she was crazy to think he would ever fall in love with her. But tonight, as he'd talked about his grief and shared things about his life that he probably never shared with others, she'd felt closer to him than she'd ever felt to any man.

"I understand that you're afraid to try again. But you needn't feel alone, Tag. I'm just as afraid as you are. But I—" Feeling more emboldened than she had a right to be, she wrapped her hands over his forearms and pressed her fingers into his warm flesh. "I'm willing to take a chance that you're not purposely setting out to break my heart."

He groaned. "Oh, Emily-Ann, I—that would never be my intention." Reaching up, he gently touched a forefinger to the center of her lips. "You've already had too much pain and hurt in your life. And so have I."

The cold fear around her heart began to melt and spread warmth to every part of her body. And then with her gaze locked on his, she placed a soft butterfly kiss upon his finger.

He whispered her name and then he was drawing her into his arms and lowering his mouth down to hers.

He'd kissed her before and each time the intimate contact had shaken her, but this time was different. This time she felt a connection that was boundless and far too strong to break.

By the time he eventually lifted his head and looked down at her, Emily-Ann was not only breathless, she was totally on fire for him.

"I think it's time we—uh—went in. Don't you?"

Without hesitating, she nodded and he quickly rose to his feet and helped her up from the swing. Then with his hand wrapped tightly around hers, he led her into the house and down a dark hallway until they passed through a door on the left.

"Wait here and I'll turn on a lamp," he said as they stepped just inside the dark room.

Emily-Ann stood where she was and while she waited for him to cross the room and deal with the light, she could feel her heart beating hard and heavy in her chest. Not with the fear of what they were about to do, but the concern that he might find her terribly disappointing. If that happened, she'd most likely never see him again.

If sex is all he wants from you, Emily-Ann, then you don't need him.

A soft light suddenly glowed at the head of a queen-size bed and then Taggart turned and smiled at her. And that was all it took to send the taunting voice, along with every other doubt, flying out of her head.

"Don't look at all the boxes that still need to be unpacked," he said.

Emily-Ann didn't bother glancing around at the room. Her focus was zeroed on him as she walked over and slipped her arms around his waist.

"Who cares about boxes?" she asked, turning her lips up to his.

Growling with need, he bent his head and kissed her. "All I care about is you. And this."

While his lips feasted on hers, his hand reached to the back of her dress and tugged on the zipper until it reached the bottom. Emily-Ann dropped her arms and allowed the fabric to slide over her shoulders and onto the floor. Cool air wafted over her half-naked body, but before it had a chance to chill her skin, he was lifting her off her feet and placing her in the middle of the bed.

Once she was settled, he stepped back and with hungry eyes she watched him remove his clothing. By the time he got down to a pair of black boxers and climbed onto the bed to join her, Emily-Ann knew her fate for tonight was sealed. Even if a thousand horses suddenly stampeded through the bedroom, she couldn't have left his side to save herself.

Chapter Nine

His body already on fire for her, Taggart rolled Emily-Ann into his arms and buried his face in the side of her neck. She smelled sweet and mysterious and the scent acted on his senses as much as the feel of her soft skin beneath his lips.

Making love to Emily-Ann had been in the back of his mind almost from the very first time he'd met her. But he'd not thought it would actually happen tonight. He'd hoped, but not believed.

Now that she was in his arms, her bare skin sliding against his, her sighs whispering across his ear, he was half-afraid he was going to wake up from a beautiful dream and find he was still in a bedroll out on the range.

"Aren't you going to turn out the light?" she asked.

Lifting his head slightly away from hers, he looked down to see her lashes were partially lowered over drowsy green eyes, while her oh-so-soft lips were already swollen from his kisses. She looked utterly fascinating. Especially to a man who only a few weeks ago believed his libido had crawled away to die.

"In a bit. Right now I want to be able to see you—how beautiful you look lying on this old quilt with your red hair spilled everywhere." He slipped his fingers beneath the lacy white straps of her bra and slid them downward until they fell onto her arms and the fleshy mounds of her breasts spilled over the loosened cups of her bra. "And I have a feeling you're going to look even better without these pretty little pieces of lace."

Her breathless little laugh was self-mocking. "There's nothing little about me or my lingerie."

"Everything about you is perfect to me, Emily-Ann. From the freckles on your nose to your rounded bottom."

She chuckled. "You're crazy."

"If I am, then please don't try to fix me. I want to stay this way."

At the middle of her back, he unfastened her bra,

then tossed the whole thing aside. The pale pink nipples of her breasts beckoned to him and, cupping his hands around the soft fullness, he bent his head to taste the rosy centers.

In a matter of seconds, she was making mewing sounds deep in her throat, while her body arched up to his. Her wordless plea for relief didn't go unnoticed. He quickly peeled off her panties and tossed them atop her dress on the floor.

When his finger found the intimate folds between her thighs, it was hot and moist and waiting just for him. Watching her face, he slipped inside and reveled at the softness he was touching, the longing he saw gripping her features.

Slowly, he stroked her until her hips were writhing against his hand and his own body was on the verge of exploding.

"Tag, oh Tag. Don't make me wait to have you."

Moving away from her, he stood and pushed off his boxers. His manhood was throbbing to be inside her and yet a part of him was reluctant to make the ultimate connection. Once he entered her, it would be the beginning of the end, and he didn't want that to happen. Not when each second of being with her like this was awakening every cell in his body.

"Is something wrong?" she asked.

Shaking away his thoughts, he pulled open the drawer in the nightstand, then frowned. "No. It's just now dawned on me that I might not have any condoms. I—they're not something—I have much need for."

She must've heard the embarrassment in his voice, because suddenly she was sitting on the side of the bed, reaching for his hand.

"No need to worry. I take the pill. Everything should be fine. Unless you're worried about—other things."

He looked at her while wishing they didn't have to discuss such an awkward subject.

"If you're worried," he said. "I can tell you that I've not had unprotected sex since I was married."

"Well, you shouldn't worry about me. I've *never* had unprotected sex."

The impish smile on her face made all the clumsiness of the moment go away and with a wicked chuckle, he eased her back down on the bed.

"Then we don't have a thing to worry about—except making this our night," he said.

Her eyes sparkling like stars, she reached up and linked her hands at the back of his neck, then drew his mouth down to hers. Taggart kissed her softly over and over until the need to deepen the kiss was as strong as the need to join his body to hers.

As soon as her mouth opened to accept his tongue, his knee parted her thighs and he entered her with one smooth thrust.

A moan vibrated deep in her throat and her hands

tightened on his shoulders, but other than that, she went stock-still beneath him.

The reaction caused him to lift his head and he was stunned to see tears slipping from the corners of her eyes and roll into the edge of her hair.

Uncertain, he whispered, "Emily-Ann, do you want to end this now?"

Her hands reached up and gently cradled his face and all he could see in her eyes was a longing so deep and tender that it caused a wave of emotion to flood the center of his chest.

"Oh, Tag, I never want this to end," she murmured. "I want you so much. So much."

He struggled to push his words past the tight cords in his throat, but when they did finally release, relief poured out with them. "And I want you, sweet Emily-Ann. More than you could know."

Lowering his head, he kissed the tears away from each corner of her eyes, then moved his mouth to hers.

The moment their lips connected, she arched her hips up to his, drawing him deeper inside her. Sensations such as he had never experienced shot at him from all directions and wiped his mind of everything but her. Having her, loving her.

Her legs wrapped around his and she instantly began to match his rhythmic thrusts. After that, his mind became a blur as his senses tried to absorb everything at once. The hot smoothness of her skin against his, the womanly scent that swirled around him, the sweetness of her lips and the yielding of her body as she gave everything up to him.

Time became nonexistent for Taggart. All he knew was that he didn't want the euphoria to end. He couldn't allow it to end. But she thwarted his plans when she began to writhe in abandon and her fingers raced frantically across his back, then down to his hips.

When she urged him to quicken the pace, it was more than his brain could stand and the rest of his body had no choice but to surrender. Suddenly and totally, he was blinded by a shower of shooting stars and then he was clutching her tightly to him, crying her name and letting the undulating waves of passion overtake him.

This wasn't the way it was supposed to be, Taggart thought a few minutes later, as he drew Emily-Ann's warm limp body next to his. He wasn't supposed to be feeling all mushy and enchanted just because he'd had sex with a woman.

Sex. Who was he trying to fool? The union they'd just shared had been far more than physical. It had touched him somewhere deep inside and now all he wanted to do was gather her close and let his heart sing with joyous wonder.

He was in trouble. Deep, deep trouble.

That dire thought was suddenly interrupted as

she stirred and nuzzled her nose against the side of his neck. He slipped his arm around her waist and snugged her next to his damp body.

"You never did turn off the lamp."

After the wild, stormy ride the two of them had just taken together, her observation caused him to chuckle.

Resting his cheek against the crown of her head, he said, "I didn't have the time. Besides, I like being able to see you."

Her fingertips created tiny circles across his chest and he wondered why her hands felt so magical whenever and wherever she touched him.

Her voice drowsy, she said, "I dreaded for you to see me without my clothes. But you know what, after a bit I didn't care."

"I think somewhere in that remark you were giving me a compliment."

"I am," she said. "You made me forget my imperfections."

He caught her hand and lifted her fingers to his lips. After he'd kissed each one, he said, "I don't know how you see yourself, Emily-Ann. But I see you as lovely and womanly and everything a man could want."

"I wasn't fishing for compliments. But—" she tilted her head in order to plant a kiss on his jaw "—I'll take them and wrap them up with a bow and put them away in my dresser. I might need them later when I'm looking in the mirror."

Smiling, he rubbed his cheek against the side of her head. "Oh, Emily-Ann, you're so—"

"Silly?"

"No. I was thinking more like precious." He turned her face to his and as he looked into her eyes, fear suddenly niggled the back of his mind.

He was feeling too much, he told himself, and thinking things that he had no business thinking. Getting this close to Emily-Ann was like asking for trouble. But he wasn't going to dwell on the danger now, not when everything about her made him feel so good.

"Tag, you don't have to say all these nice things to me," she said. "I don't expect that from you."

He inwardly winced. "I never thought you did. But I need to say them. And maybe someday you'll realize I actually mean them."

Doubt shrouded her green eyes and he was amazed at how much he wanted to take the dark shadows away. And stunned even more to realize how much he wanted her to believe in him.

A vulnerable quiver touched her bottom lip. "I want to believe them, Tag. I want to believe everything about this night."

He pushed his fingers into the hair at her temple and stroked the silky strands away from her face.

"I'm glad," he whispered. "Because it's far from over."

The tremble to her lips stopped as the corners tilted upward. "Just so I get to work at Conchita's by six thirty in the morning."

He gave her a wicked grin. "I'll give you enough time to make the drive."

Her provocative laugh had him laughing along with her and with a hand on her waist, he rolled the both of them over, until he was lying on his back and her warm body was draped over his.

And when she lowered her head and covered his mouth with hers, Taggart realized he wanted to believe everything about this night, too.

Two days later, Emily-Ann had closed up the coffee shop and was climbing into her car to drive home when Camille's truck pulled up behind her.

Sticking her head out the window, her friend called out to her, "Not so fast! I just got here!"

Giving her a cheery wave, Emily-Ann left the side of the car and walked over to greet Camille.

"What are you doing in town so late in the evening?" she asked, as Camille climbed down from the truck cab.

"Mother sent me after a few personal items she needed from the drugstore. Personally, I think she sent me on this mission to give me a chance to see you."

"Oh, she thought you needed someone other than relatives for company?"

"Something like that." She glanced over Emily-Ann's shoulder to see she'd already hung the closed sign on the door of the coffee shop. "Were you on your way home? Or were you going somewhere?"

"Home. I have another test to do tomorrow and it deals with chemistry. I've been studying between customers, but I need some uninterrupted time to study if I ever expect to pass." Plus, it was damned hard to keep her mind on chemical equations when all she really wanted to think about was Taggart and how the night at his house had changed everything.

Camille groaned with disappointment. "Don't you have time to go to the Broken Spur for a milkshake?"

Emily-Ann frowned. "No more milkshakes for me—I'm cutting back. And why do you want to go to that old café on the outskirts of town? There's a fast-food place a couple of streets over from here where you can get a milkshake."

Camille's short burst of laughter was a mocking sound. "Are you joking? The Broken Spur might be a little ratty on the inside, but the food is great. Makes me feel right at home like I'm in my own diner. And they make their milkshakes by hand one at a time. With real ice cream."

Chuckling, Emily-Ann affectionately patted Camille's protruding belly. "And the little guy is growing. He deserves the real thing."

"Darned right," Camille agreed. "So what do you say? I won't keep you for more than thirty minutes. I need to get back to the ranch soon anyway. Mom wants this new lipstick I picked up for her. Uncle Gil is taking her out to dinner tonight."

Emily-Ann's looked at her with interest. "Really? Is she calling it a date?"

Camille shrugged. "I don't know what Mom is calling the outing, but I can tell you that she's awfully excited about it."

"Aww, that's so romantic," Emily-Ann replied, then suddenly realized that kind of remark might not go over well with Camille. "Sorry, Camille. I spoke before I thought. You might not want to think of your mother having a romantic evening."

"Don't be silly," she said with a dismissive wave of her hand. "I've already told you that I want Mother to be happy. And if that means having Uncle Gil in her life, then that's okay, too."

"Not all children feel as generous toward their parent as you do."

Camille smiled wistfully. "How could I want to deny her the pleasure of loving someone when I have so much with Matthew?"

"True. And you don't have to worry about Gil being like Gorman, thank God," she said, then called over her shoulder as she started to her car, "Okay. Let me get my purse and we'll go to the Broken Spur. I'll have an ice tea while you enjoy *real* ice cream."

Camille drove the two of them to the far south side of town where the old Broken Spur building sat on the edge of the highway that led to Phoenix. The place was usually full of old cowboys and construction workers and today was no different, Emily-Ann decided, as she and Camille sat in a corner booth, sipping their drinks.

"Camille, I swear, each time I see you it's like your face is glowing. Have you found some sort of miracle moisturizer, or something?"

Camille chuckled. "When a woman gets overloaded with hormones, she not only cries, but she has much nicer skin. This glow will go away once I have little junior or baby princess."

Emily-Ann sighed. For the past few years she'd watched the Hollister women give birth to several babies and each time she'd been very happy for them. And when she'd heard that Camille was expecting Matthew's child, she'd been thrilled for her friend. Yet she'd never really allowed herself to dwell on the idea of having her own children. The notion had never seemed to fit her life. Not without a good man in it. But now, after making love to Taggart, she was imagining herself more and more with a baby.

"Actually, I'd better fess up," Camille went on. "Mother did want the new lipstick for tonight, but she also sent me into town on a nosy, fact-finding mission. And I agreed because I'm really curious, too."

Emily-Ann asked blankly, "Curious about what?

I didn't know anything new had been happening around here."

Her expression innocent, Camille stirred the straw through the creamy strawberry milkshake. "According to Isabelle something has been happening. She told Holt that Tag cooked supper for you the other night. And you know Holt, you'd have to duct tape his mouth before he could keep it shut."

Emily-Ann couldn't stop a pink blush from coloring her cheeks. "Well, no need to beat up Holt. It's not like we were trying to be secretive or anything."

Camille's blue eyes were suddenly sparkling with interest and she leaned earnestly across the tabletop toward Emily-Ann. "Good. I want to hear all about it. So does Mother."

Maureen had always been like a second mother to Emily-Ann, but she couldn't remember a time that the woman had actually been interested in her dates.

"Why is she interested? The dinner was—well, just a casual outing."

"Do you want your nose to look like a carrot?" She grimaced. "With fibs like that it's going to."

Emily-Ann shifted uncomfortably on the padded vinyl covering the booth bench. There was no way she could tell her friend that she'd experienced something with Taggart that had been totally magical and life changing for her. She'd not had any idea that having sex with a man could make her feel so wanted and loved and needed. She'd not known that she was capable of feeling that much pleasure or that much emotion. But she had. And two days later she still didn't know where their relationship was headed or what any of it might mean on down the line.

"Okay, I'll admit it was more than special." Shaking her head, she momentarily closed her eyes. "Camille, I never thought—well, can you imagine a man like Taggart cooking supper for me? If it hadn't actually happened it would be downright laughable."

"Why?"

Emily-Ann's eyes flew wide. "Why? Are you kidding? Think about it, Camille. I'm the girl that was fed a sandwich from a convenience store for her twenty-seventh birthday and I had to eat that meal sitting in the car in the parking lot because my date had an aversion to picnic tables. I've never been treated as nicely as Taggart treats me."

A wide smile came over Camille's face and she reached across the table and squeezed Emily-Ann's hand. "That's wonderful."

Emily-Ann let out a heavy breath. "I'm not so sure if it is or not."

"Now who's sounding like they've slipped a cog or two?"

"I realize that sounds crazy. But that's because you don't understand, Camille. When something or someone as good as Taggart comes along in my life I'm fairly certain I'm destined to end up a loser—again. He's not going to want to invest much more time in me. And he especially won't want to invest any true emotion."

"That's an awful thing to say, Emily-Ann. Don't you think you're doing Taggart a discredit by thinking that way?"

Emily-Ann sighed again. "I'm trying to be practical about this, Camille. He—uh—he's already told me he doesn't think he can make a long-term commitment to me—or any woman. You see, he—" Unsure as to whether she should say more, Emily-Ann paused and glanced down at the tabletop. "Well, let's just say he's not looking for love."

"Don't most men say those things? Matthew tried his best to run from me. But in the end he decided that marrying me was a chance he had to take."

Grimacing, Emily-Ann lifted her tea glass and drew on the straw. "Yes, well, Matthew had good reason to be gun-shy. He'd been through a divorce. And Taggart has good reason to be leery of loving again. He—" Pausing, she shook her head, then seeing Camille was waiting for her to continue, she said, "I'm not sure I should be repeating this. But he didn't ask me to keep it a secret."

"You don't have to tell me anything private about you and Taggart. Not unless you want to," Camille assured her.

The thought of what he'd gone through had continued to revolve through her mind, haunting her with images of his loss and pain.

Pinching the bridge of her nose, she said, "Maybe he's told Blake or someone in your family about this. I don't know. He didn't say. But he was married once—years ago. His wife and unborn child were killed in a car accident."

Camille looked genuinely stricken. "Oh, how completely horrible."

"Yes. And not only that, his mother died three months later. From what he told me, he was very close to her and losing all of them so close together has sort of warped his heart, I guess you'd say."

"No doubt. But time heals. We both know that. And none of that means he's incapable of falling in love again—with you," Camille argued. "After all, what man couldn't fall in love with you?"

The absurdity of Camille's question caused Emily-Ann to laugh outright. "Oh, sure. Men have been knocking down my door for years," she said with sarcastic humor.

"Well, you have one on your doorstep now. A good one. What do you intend to do about it? Mother happens to believe you and Taggart make a perfect match. Should I tell her that you think so, too?"

Emily-Ann groaned, then looked across the room to where a row of men sat at a worn bar eating pie and drinking coffee. The image reminded her even more of Taggart scarfing up the pecan pie that Reeva had made for him. He'd eaten the dessert with the same enthusiasm he'd made love to her.

Swallowing hard, she turned her gaze back to Camille. "Tell your mother that it's going to take more than a bridal bouquet for Taggart to fall in love with me."

The horses were tired, prompting Taggart and Matthew to pull them to a slow walk as they traveled the last half mile back to the ranch yard.

"The grass is looking good," Matthew said. "The cows are all settled where they need to be and the branding and vaccinating is all finished. I think it's about time Camille and I head back home to Red Bluff. You have everything under control here."

Taggart let out a cynical grunt, but his reaction had very little to do with being foreman of Three Rivers Ranch. He could truthfully say he felt confident about his job, with or without Matthew here to guide him. But as for his personal life, it was totally out of control.

Even if taking Emily-Ann into his bed had been the most incredible experience he'd ever had, it was still a stupid mistake on his part. He should've known that once he touched her, he'd only want more. He should've known that he couldn't just have sex with her, then walk away. No. She was meant to be made love to and he was very much afraid that's exactly what he'd done. Now his brain, his heart, his very being was consumed with her. And he didn't have a clue as to what he was going to do about it.

"I can't speak for Camille, but I'd be willing to say you'll be glad to get back to your own ranch."

This time it was Matthew who grunted. "For years, if anyone had told me I'd be looking forward to leaving Three Rivers for Red Bluff, I would've considered them crazy. Three Rivers was my very lifeblood. But things change. Most of the time in ways a man never expects."

Taggart understood that only too well. And in his own case, the changes weren't good. "Guess you're talking about your wife now," he said, as he absently flipped the ends of the split reins back and forth across the cantle of the saddle.

"Yeah. Nothing would mean much of anything without her and the coming baby. I'm building Red Bluff for them."

"Must be nice."

"Nice, hell. The feeling it gives me is impossible to describe." He glanced over at Taggart. "And frankly, I never imagined myself being this blessed. Sometimes it's scary because I never had much in the way of family. My mother died when my sister and I were young. After that we were sent to live with an uncle that was a real bastard. Finding the Hollisters and loving Camille is sometimes too good to believe. You understand what I'm trying to say."

"More than you could know, Matthew. My mother died, too, when I was in my midtwenties. And Dad— he's not worth talking about. I don't have a loving wife to share things with, but landing here on Three Rivers is more than I ever expected in my life."

"Yeah. I guess being here does feel pretty good to you."

Making his home on Three Rivers and being with Emily-Ann had changed his life drastically. And those good changes were scary. But he wasn't a timid little calf, afraid to follow his mama to greener pastures, Taggart mentally argued with himself. Sure, he'd suffered through some tragedies, but he'd come out on the other side a bit wiser and hopefully stronger. And a man couldn't go forward if he continually held on to the past.

"It feels damned good, Matthew," he finally replied.

For the next few minutes, the two men rode on down the well-trodden cattle trail in companionable silence until Matthew abruptly pulled his horse to a stop and climbed down from the saddle.

Taggart reined his buckskin next to Matthew's horse. "Anything wrong?" he asked.

"No. I'll be right back."

He walked a few steps off the trail and snapped off a long bough of blooming sage. After he climbed back into the saddle, he looked over at Taggart and grinned.

"Camille loves this stuff. It grows everywhere like annoying weeds, but she thinks it's beautiful and special. Go figure." He held up the branch with silver-green leaves and tiny purple blooms. "This will make her happy."

"You're a smart guy, Matthew."

The other man chuckled as he nudged his horse into a walk. "Not smart enough."

No, Taggart thought, a man could be a genius and still not be able to understand a woman. The tears he'd seen in Emily-Ann's eyes when they'd begun to make love had puzzled him. He'd kept wondering what she could've been thinking to put them there.

She hadn't been thinking, Taggart. She'd been feeling. Those tears had come straight from her heart. But you don't want to face that kind of truth. You don't want to think that Emily-Ann could feel that much for you. That would make everything more complicated and painful when it ended. Right?

Shoving at the nagging voice, Taggart glanced over at Matthew and the bough of sage he'd laid across the front of the saddle seat.

The foreman of Red Bluff was more like him than Taggart could've guessed. He'd not been born into wealth and from what he'd just said, his growing-up years had been far from easy. And along the way, he'd lost loved ones. Yet he'd found the courage to give his heart to a woman, to marry her and plan a future.

Could he be that brave? Taggart asked himself. Or was he going to keep on hiding his heart and hoping that Emily-Ann couldn't find it?

Chapter Ten

Emily-Ann leaned back from the computer monitor and rubbed her weary eyes. Ever since she'd gotten home from her outing with Camille at the Broken Spur, she'd been sitting at the tiny desk set up in her bedroom. That had been three hours ago. Now her eyes were burning and her shoulders felt like they were permanently locked in one painful position.

She was shutting down the computer and switching off a table lamp when her cell phone dinged with an incoming message.

Seeing it was from Taggart, she quickly grabbed up the phone and scanned the brief note.

Don't eat. I'll be there in thirty minutes.

Her heart tapping a rapid thud against her chest, she lowered the phone and stared unseeingly at the wall in front of her.

Taggart was coming to see her tonight? Only two days had passed since she'd gone to his place for supper. She'd not expected him to want to see her again this soon. What did it mean? That he was actually beginning to care about her? Or he was simply wanting another round of sex?

It was pointless to ask herself those questions. No matter the answers, she couldn't resist the man.

Focusing on the phone in her hand, she tapped a one-word reply.

Okay.

Thirty minutes later after pulling on a pair of faded blue jeans and a red peasant blouse, she dabbed on a small amount of makeup and added a pair of silver hoops to her ears before she hurried to the living room to pick up the clutter.

She'd barely had time to carry a couple of dirty cups and a stack of junk mail to the kitchen when she heard Taggart's footsteps on the porch.

When she opened the door, he was standing on the threshold grinning back at her. Dressed in jeans and a blue denim shirt worn through in several places, he was holding a sack in each arm. The scent of fried food wafted toward her.

"Is that chicken I smell?" she asked, as she motioned him into the house.

The grin still on his face, he moved into the living room. "Since we ate beef the other night at my place, I thought you might like a change," he told her.

After dealing with the door, she crossed to where he was standing. "You didn't need to bring food. I would've made something for you," she said, then chuckled. "Uh—but you were probably afraid I'd give you cold cuts again."

"I love cold cuts," he insisted. "I just wanted to treat you."

Seeing him again was causing bubbles of joy to dance around inside of her and she didn't think twice about rising on the tips of her toes and pressing a kiss on his cheek.

"I'm so happy you're here, Tag. And thank you for the treat—whatever it is," she said, then gestured toward the kitchen. "Let's take it to the table."

He started toward the kitchen and Emily-Ann followed along at his side.

"Sorry about the short notice that I was coming," he said. "I hope you didn't have other plans."

"You mean like stare at the walls?" she teased, then shook her head. "No plans. In fact, I just finished studying for the night. I'm all set for my chemistry test."

"I'm glad it's you and not me. I was fairly good with math, but chemistry usually got me confused. Now Doc can rattle off all those different elements and medicines used to treat animals like he's talking about what he likes for breakfast."

"Chandler is a brain, plain and simple," Emily-Ann said.

They entered the kitchen and he placed the large paper sacks on the table. "I stopped by the clinic before I headed over here and Doc removed the stitches from my arm. He also gave me a warning to go with the service," he said.

"Oh, what was the warning?" she asked curiously, while thinking Chandler had probably warned Taggart to stay away from her. Not that the veterinarian was a snob. He was far from it. And he truly was Emily-Ann's friend. But that didn't mean he thought she'd be the right woman for their new foreman.

"That I quit playing with Holt's yearlings," Taggart answered.

Emily-Ann laughed. "Good advice."

His expression suddenly changed from playful to coy as he reached inside one of the sacks and pulled out a bunch of white tulips mixed with some sort of vivid pink flowers she'd never seen before. The bouquet was beautiful and obviously expensive.

"For you," he said gently. "I hope you like tulips."

Clasping the bouquet with both hands, she stared

down at the blooms in stunned fascination. "I love tulips. I—"

Her words broke off as the tears clogging her throat made it impossible to speak.

Embarrassed by the overemotional reaction, she turned and hurried over to the sink. With her back turned to Taggart, she placed the flowers on the cabinet counter and attempted to wipe the tears that were suddenly rolling down her cheeks.

When she felt his hand come down on her shoulder, she sniffed and desperately tried to compose herself.

"Sorry, Tag. The way I'm acting you're probably thinking I never received flowers from a man before. And you'd be right. I haven't."

He didn't reply and, when his silence continued, Emily-Ann figured he was feeling worse than awkward. He was probably kicking himself for becoming involved with a woman who'd never so much as merited a bouquet of flowers.

Clearing her throat, she stepped away from the hold he had on her shoulder and walked to the opposite end of the cabinet to look for something to hold the bouquet. After a moment of digging around in a bottom shelf, she pulled out a pitcher made of blue knobby milk glass.

"I'll put the flowers in some water," she told him. "And then I'll set the table so we can eat. We don't want the food to get cold after you went to the trouble and expense of buying it."

She was chattering, but that was the only way she could handle his silence and keep her tears at bay at the same time.

Her attention focused solely on taking care of the bouquet, she filled the pitcher with water and dropped in the flowers. However, that was as far as she got before Taggart's hands were on her upper arms, pulling her around to face him.

"Forget the damned food," he muttered. "Forget about everything, but this."

He didn't give her time to utter any kind of question. Instead, he tugged her into his arms and fastened his mouth roughly over hers.

The contact of their lips was all it took to wipe everything from Emily-Ann's mind. All she could think about was making love to this man, who was quickly becoming everything to her.

Just as her taut nerves began to relax and her body sagged against his, he lifted his head and sucked in a ragged breath. "You don't have a clue as to how much I want you, Emily-Ann."

Her hands gripped the front of his denim shirt as she tilted her head back to look up at him. "But I thought—"

"You're always thinking too much," he interrupted.

Lowering her lashes, she looked up at him with

a properly chastised expression. "And talking too much," she said, unable to stop the corners of her mouth from bending upward. "Aren't you going to tack that on, too?"

"No." His smile a little wicked, his hands slipped to the rounded curve of her bottom and pulled her hips forward until they were snug against his. "I have other ways to keep you from talking."

Her arms slipped up around his neck. "I'd like for you to show me those—other ways."

"It'll be my pleasure, sweet Emily-Ann."

Taking him by the hand, she led him through the small house until they reached her bedroom.

"I don't think we need a light this time," she said as she urged him toward the double bed covered in a white chenille bedspread. "The streetlight shines through the slats of the blinds."

"I wouldn't care if we were in the blaring sunlight or the deepest blackest night, I'd want you just as much," he said.

"I'll be honest, Tag, I didn't expect to see you again this soon." Even as she said the words, her hands were reaching for the front of his shirt, pulling the snaps apart. "You've made me happy."

He pushed her hair aside and pressed a track of kisses up the side of her neck and onto her ear. "Mmm. I'll try my best to make you even happier."

Seconds ticked by as he showered kisses upon her face and lips, then down the creamy column of her throat. When his mouth finally reached the cleavage between her breasts, he lifted his head and went to work removing her clothes.

By the time he got down to her bra and panties, her breaths had gone short and rapid, while her heart was pounding, drumming out a rhythm that he and he alone controlled.

"Tag, I don't think you—you're not supposed to be making me feel this good," she whispered hoarsely. "It's decadent. And scary. And addictive."

He groaned. "It's not me that's making this magic. It's us. Together."

With her lingerie off and out of the way, he eased her onto the bed, then quickly shed his own clothing and joined her in the middle of the mattress.

She reached to wrap her arms around him and as his mouth found hers, his hands began a slow foray of her body, pausing at certain parts to tug and tease, until the fire inside her began to burn hotter than an Arizona wildfire. She did her best to reciprocate the pleasure by soothing her fingers over his broad shoulders, down his rib cage and onto his back.

Between them she could feel his hard erection pressing against her belly and the evidence of his desire emboldened her to give everything to him and take exactly what she wanted.

He continued to kiss her over and over and each time the connection grew deeper until she was certain their breaths had braided into one life-giving function. Thinking became nonexistent as her senses scattered like a covey of birds flying in every direction. All she knew was that Taggart wanted her and she wanted him with every cell of her being.

And when he finally rolled her onto her back and coupled his body with hers, Emily-Ann felt, for the first time in her life, that she was totally and truly complete.

Much later, after Taggart had gathered enough energy to open his eyes, he noticed the cover at the foot of the double bed was striped with artificial light streaming through the blinds. Alongside him, Emily-Ann was lying on her back, her breasts rising and falling as she slowly regained her breath.

Across the small room, on the wall directly in front of the bed, a partially raised window allowed the cool night air to drift over them. The breeze carried no scent of sage or juniper. And though he caught the sound of barking dogs and distant traffic, there was no bawling cows, nickering horses or wailing coyotes.

Next to him, Emily-Ann stirred and slipped an arm across his waist.

In a drowsy voice, she asked, "What are you thinking?"

"How different it feels to be in town." Which was true enough, he thought. But he couldn't tell her all the other things that were swirling around in his mind. Like how the simple touch of her hand turned him inside out and how being with her had become a very important part of his life.

"Hmm. Well, you're not a town guy," she remarked, then rose up on one elbow and looked down at his face. "I've been wondering something about you."

A wry grin slanted his lips. "What's that? If I've ever spent time in jail?"

She chuckled. "The possibility never crossed my mind. But I'll bet you'd look good in orange."

He couldn't help but laugh and when his gaze found her sweet face in the semidarkness, he felt everything inside him go soft and gooey.

"What have you been wondering?"

With her free hand, she trailed fingers up and down the length of his arm. "Where you learned about ranching? How you came to be a cowboy?"

He drew in a long breath, then blew it out in a rough sigh. "From my maternal grandfather and my father. When I was a little kid, my sister and I and our parents all lived with Grandad Walt on his ranch near Hereford. So I grew up learning all about being a cowboy and caring for livestock."

Her brows pulled together. "Oh. Didn't you tell me before that your father was a carpenter?"

"That was several years later," he explained. "See, Grandad Walt died suddenly and willed the ranch to his sister. So we all had to move out. When that happened Dad went to work on the Flying W."

She stared at him in wonder. "Your grandfather didn't consider leaving the ranch to his daughter—your mother? Seems like that would've been the logical thing. Especially with your whole family already living there."

Taggart snorted cynically. "Are you kidding? Grandad couldn't stand Dad. He only tolerated his son-in-law because of his daughter. And to be fair, he knew what my father would do with the place if it went to Mom. Dad would've wrung every dollar he could from it, then let it go to ruin. No, Grandad made the right choice."

Frowning, she said, "Wait a minute. Did you say your father went to work on the Flying W? Isn't that—"

"Yeah. The ranch where I worked before I moved to Three Rivers. Doesn't sound right, but it's true. Several years after they fired Dad, I wanted to get away from the monotony of the feedlot job and asked the family with the Flying W to hire me. I was fortunate. The Williamsons didn't hold it against me because of Dad's shiftless attitude. You see, he didn't like taking orders. Nor did he want to do anything that required him to get off his horse—like mending fences, repairing broken windmills, or whatever needed to be done on the ground."

"What a terrible waste—on your father's part, I

mean," she said. "Sounds like he had plenty of good opportunities and blew them."

Talking about his father's shortcomings had never been easy for Taggart, but he learned with Emily-Ann he didn't need to sugarcoat the facts. He could be honest and not have to worry about her being judgmental.

He said, "Well, selfish people tend to squander anything that's worthwhile."

"Hmm. Sad, but true." She eased her head onto his shoulder. "I witnessed plenty of squandering in my family, Tag, and I don't want to be guilty of doing it. Especially with you."

Sliding his hand against her back, he threaded his fingers in her long hair. It was still damp from the exertion of their lovemaking and when he lifted the strands to his lips, the scent was a reminder of all the soft and tender things he'd missed these past years.

No. He didn't want to squander this precious time with Emily-Ann, he thought. He wanted to hold on to it—to her—as long as this thing between them continued to hold together.

"You know, we have food waiting for us in the kitchen," he murmured.

"Mmm. And my beautiful flowers, too." She tilted her head just enough to allow her gaze to settle on his face. "Tag, the flowers—I didn't mean to cry. The tears came before I could stop them—because I was so touched that you thought of me in that way.

And I was thinking, too, that all through my mother's life, she never received a single flower from a man. She was a good woman. She deserved better—but I could only think that I didn't deserve better than her. Does that make sense to you?"

He tightened his arm across her back and drew her closer to his side.

"Sorry, but it doesn't make sense," he said gently. "You're a good woman, too. And you're not your mother. Just like I'm not like any of those guys who've disappointed you in the past."

She studied his face for long moments and then she asked, "Do you think we could forget about the food for a little while? Right now I need to kiss your lips. I want to make sure they really did say I was a good woman."

Cupping his hand at the back of her head, he drew her face upward until the tip of his nose was brushing hers. "Right now my lips are going to say the food can be reheated."

With a lusty chuckle, she curled her arm around his neck. "I can be, too."

The morning sun was just beginning to peep over the eastern hills as Taggart watched the cowboys form groups of two and three as they headed in different directions across the ranch yard. The work orders he'd just given the men for the day had all been received with smiles and good-natured jokes.

Since he'd taken over the job of foreman, not one had grumbled or griped about the task he'd assigned them. Taggart liked to think the men were cooperative because they approved of him being their new foreman. Yet he realized they'd all been handpicked by the Hollisters and most of them had been here on Three Rivers Ranch for years. Some even before Taggart had been born. They weren't the type of men to slough off or complain.

The thought caused his mind to drift back to the night he'd taken Emily-Ann the flowers and he'd talked to her about his father and the problems the man had caused his family. Something had happened to him that night. He'd felt a connection to Emily-Ann that was unlike anything he'd ever experienced before. It had filled him with warm contentment and a sense of homecoming. Now, more than two weeks later, he was still trying to figure out exactly what those feelings meant and how he was going to hold on to them—and her.

Walking over to the horse he'd saddled for his personal use today, he tried to put Emily-Ann out of his mind for the moment. He had work to do and she was coming out to the ranch to see him tonight. He'd let himself concentrate on her then.

Hell, he'd do more than concentrate, he thought. Once he had her in his arms, he wouldn't be letting her go until the wee hours of the morning.

And do you honestly believe having sex is all the

woman wants from you, Taggart? Could be that she's just like all other women. She might want to be wined and dined and taken somewhere other than to bed. But then, you don't really care about what she wants, do you? You say you don't want to be like the other men she's had in her life, but that's a laugh. You need to take a long look in the mirror and make yourself face the truth.

Doing his best to block out the caustic voice going off in his head, he got busy tightening the cinch strap on the saddle. With that task finished, he was checking the rest of the tack when the cell phone in his pocket pinged with a new message.

Thinking it might be Blake wanting him to stop by the office, he pulled out the phone and was a bit surprised to see a message so early in the morning from his sister, Tallulah.

To give you a heads-up—Dad has been coming around, asking for money. I haven't given him any. But he's making noises about coming out there to see you. Guess he thinks you're rich now. She ended the message with a heart emoji, along with a smiley face.

Hearing from his sister usually gave Taggart a happy lift, but this warning about their father was unsettling. Damn it. The man was a user and Taggart wanted no part of him. And he definitely didn't want the man making his sister miserable or messing up things here on Three Rivers.

"That frown on your face is about as deep as the Grand Canyon. Trouble this morning?"

Maureen's voice pulled Taggart out of his dark thoughts and he turned around to see the Hollister matriarch walking up to him. She was wearing her usual work attire of jeans and boots and an old gray felt hat pulled over her chestnut ponytail. A saddled bay horse followed close behind her right shoulder.

"No. Nothing that can't be fixed." He dropped the phone back into his shirt pocket and looked at her. "The men are just now heading out. Were you planning on joining some of them, or me?"

Smiling, she said, "Given a choice, I'll take you. I don't know what you had planned for this morning, but I thought we might take a long ride."

Questions immediately circled through Taggart's head. Normally Gil showed up with Maureen every morning and the two of them had been going out together to help with the ranching chores. But the man was clearly absent today.

"I can do that," he said. "Did you have a certain place on the ranch in mind?"

"I do. I want to ride over to water pump number nine."

Taggart stared at the woman and hoped the shock he was feeling didn't show on his face. "Maureen, I—are you sure? That's the place—"

Her lips formed a grim line. "Listen, Tag, you don't have to tiptoe around me. My sons think they need to treat me like I'm a marshmallow or something. They're wrong. Do I look soft?"

"Not exactly." On the outside she was an attractive woman, but Taggart had already learned that on the inside she was as tough as nails.

"Hell, I'm not going to fall apart if someone mentions Joel's name. Or says he was most likely murdered. I've lived with the reality of his death for years now."

"Yes, but do you think it's wise for us to ride to that area? Does anyone, other than me, know what you have planned?"

She scowled at him. "No. And I don't intend on telling any of them. I don't want to hear all their arguments and excuses to try to stop me. As far as anyone knows, you and I are going out to check on a herd of cows. That's what I told Reeva when I left the house this morning and that's what we'll tell anyone else if they ask. Got it?"

"Got it," Taggart assured her. "We're checking on cows."

What else could he say? She was the owner of the ranch. He didn't want to go against her wishes. But the more he thought about it, the more he liked the idea that she felt she could trust him. And if he could help her, even if it was just to ease her curiosity about the area where her husband had met his demise, it would be well worth the ride.

She wasted no time swinging herself into the saddle. "I have a canteen of water," she said. "Do you?"

"I have a couple of bottles in my saddlebags."

She rolled her eyes. "You young people. Those things burst at the drop of your hat. Plus they don't keep the water cool like a canteen. I'm going to make a point to buy you one."

Grinning, Taggart finished tightening his cinch. "Yes, ma'am."

Maureen chuckled as he swung his leg over the saddle and reined his horse alongside hers.

She said, "Forgive me, Tag. I'm sounding like a mother. Sometimes I just can't help myself."

"Don't worry. I can get used to it."

For the next two hours they rode in a southerly direction, occasionally alternating the gait of the horses from a walk to a long trot.

With the ranch covering miles in all directions, Taggart still hadn't seen all there was to see of the property. But last week, he'd ridden with Joseph over to water well number nine and he'd not forgotten how to get there. The deputy was always in hopes of finding new evidence and the two of them had searched several dry gulches before they'd finally given up and headed home.

Taggart was wondering if Maureen knew about their recent trip or any of the past trips her sons had made to this area of the ranch. So far during their ride, she'd not mentioned anything about the investigation the men had been making into Joel's death, but that didn't mean she was oblivious to what had been going on.

"I imagine you've been wondering why Gil didn't show up with me today," she said, as the two of them crossed a shallow stream shaded with willows.

"It did cross my mind," Taggart admitted.

"He had to go to Phoenix today on police business. They still ask for his help sometimes on certain cases. But he doesn't plan on making a habit of going down there. He'd rather be here on the ranch."

"He seems to like doing ranch work." And being with you, Taggart could've added.

"Ranching is what he was really meant to do," she said, then glanced over at him. "I think my children and most everyone who knows me has been wondering why I invited Gil to move into the ranch house instead of getting a place of his own."

"I've not heard anyone remarking on the subject," Taggart said honestly.

She let out a short laugh. "I'm sure the subject has been beaten to death by many, but that doesn't really worry me. There are reasons I feel this way. And no. Gil and I aren't having an affair, but we are growing close. Like you and Emily-Ann, maybe?"

Her question caught him by complete surprise. Not that she knew he'd been seeing Emily-Ann, but because she'd openly asked him about it.

Knowing his expression was worse than sheepish, he wiped a hand over his face and tried to give her a genuine smile.

"We have been spending a lot of time together. She's a special woman."

"I've always known it would take a special man to see that about her. I'm glad it's you, Tag."

What would Maureen think if he told her that he'd been doing more than seeing Emily-Ann? That he was having an affair with her? Most likely, she'd be highly disappointed in him. It was obvious that Maureen thought of Emily-Ann as a third daughter and she didn't want her hurt for anyone or any reason.

Not that Taggart planned to hurt her. But he was beginning to ask himself just how far their relationship could go. In spite of how happy she made him, he still couldn't let himself think in terms of forever. He'd already learned that there was no forever. Not for him.

His troubled thoughts must have shown on his face, because Maureen suddenly asked, "What's wrong? You look awfully glum for a man who has a special woman in his life."

Lifting his hat from his head, he swiped a hand through his sweaty hair. "I haven't told anybody but Emily-Ann about this, but I was married a long time ago. She and the baby we were expecting got killed in a car crash."

"I know."

Stunned, he stared at her. He couldn't believe

Emily-Ann had divulged something he'd told her in private. "How did you know?"

The smile she gave him was gentle and reassuring. "You don't think I would allow anyone to come in and take over the foreman job at Three Rivers without learning all about him first, now do you?"

So the Hollisters had done more than read his résumé, Taggart thought. Well, he should have already realized they would do a background check on him. They ran a multimillion-dollar business. They couldn't take chances on hiring someone who might end up being dishonest.

"Oh. Well, you never mentioned anything about it to me," he reasoned.

"There wasn't any point. And I wouldn't be doing it now but I think I've become somewhat of an expert at being a widow and I know the sort of things that are probably still going through your mind— even though it's been a long time since the tragedy."

Sighing, he absently stroked the sorrel's neck. "You can't forget, Maureen. Not entirely."

"Exactly. But you can move beyond it."

Curious now, he looked at her. "Is that what you've done with Gil?"

Before she could answer, he swiftly shook his head. "I'm sorry, Maureen. I'm being too damned nosy. Just forget I asked that."

"No. I'm glad you did ask it. My answer is that I'm trying. And that's what I hope you're doing, too,

Tag. With Emily-Ann. Moving forward. Unafraid. I think you both deserve that."

He could've told her he'd been hoping for the same thing. Hoping that one day soon, he would wake up feeling like a confident man. God only knew how much he wanted to be free of the past and to be able to reach out for the things he truly wanted. But moving on took lots of courage and strength and so far he'd not been able to find those things.

Glancing ahead, he noticed they were approaching an arroyo that was so deep that cattle and horses could only climb in and out at certain places.

"We don't have very far to go to the well pump now, Maureen," Taggart told her. "If you want to turn around and go back, I'll understand."

Shaking her head, she smiled at him. "I just gave you a talk about moving forward, Tag, and that's exactly what we're going to do."

She nudged her spurs into the horse's side and the bay took off into a long trot straight toward the arroyo.

Taggart realized Maureen wasn't going to give him the option of turning around. Like it or not, he had to follow. And he suddenly wondered if this long trip had actually been taken for her sake, or his.

Chapter Eleven

Later that same day, a few short miles before the turnoff to Three Rivers Ranch, Emily-Ann passed the entrance to the Bar X where Tessa and Joseph lived with their young son, Little Joe, and baby daughter, Spring. The youngest of the Hollister brothers, he'd been the first to marry and have children. Now the men were all married with growing families and so were their sisters, Vivian and Camille. One by one, Emily-Ann had watched them find love and happiness, the kind that tied two people together for the duration of their lives. And somewhere between the weddings and showers and christenings, she'd hoped and prayed that the same sort of love and happiness would come to her.

So far it hadn't happened, and though she'd allowed her hopes to rise when she'd first met Taggart, she was beginning to accept the fact that he'd been completely honest when he told her he wasn't looking for anything long-term.

This past month the two of them had spent every possible night they could manage with each other. And when she'd been lying in his arms, he'd never as much as mentioned the word *love*, much less coupled it with the word *future*. The two of them were simply living in the moment. And she had no idea how much longer this thing between them could last.

The reality caused her to push out a heavy sigh, but it was hardly enough to make her put her foot on the brake and turn the car around. No. Being with Taggart was something she couldn't resist. He made her feel beautiful and sexy and worthy. And for now she had to hold on to the hope that one day he might actually fall in love with her.

You ninny. When are you ever going to grow up? A man like Taggart isn't ever going to fall in love with you. The only kind of man you'll ever snag is one that's afraid of his own shadow, poor as a church mouse, or so slovenly you'll have to knock his feet off the furniture. This cowboy is temporary with a capital T.

Hating the nagging voice rattling around in her

head, Emily-Ann pushed harder on the accelerator. Taggart was waiting for her and right now that was all that mattered.

Taggart was late getting home. Through the darkness he could see Emily-Ann's car already parked in her usual spot next to a patch of prickly pear. The fact that she was here to greet him lifted some of the fatigue from his shoulders.

By the time he reached the steps to the porch, he spotted her sitting in the wooden swing. King was up in the seat, lying with his head on her lap.

"So much for King being a big, tough working dog," he joked. "It's no wonder he wants to stay here instead of the ranch yard—where he belongs."

Smiling, she stroked the dog's head. "With a name like his, he's supposed to be treated like royalty."

"Hmm. I think I'll change mine to prince." Grinning, he sauntered over to the swing. "Maybe I'll get more kisses that way."

"Hah!"

Easing the dog's head off her lap, she stood, wrapped her arms around Taggart's waist and planted a soft kiss on his lips. "Hello, Prince."

The sweetness of her greeting pushed away the troubling thoughts that had drifted in and out of his head all day and he gladly kissed her again. Just to make sure they didn't reappear to ruin this night for him.

"Sorry I'm so late. You should have gone on in the house. Have you been here long?"

"Not too long," she answered. "And don't worry, I've already been inside. I brought food."

Curving his arm around her shoulders, he urged her toward the door. Behind them, King lifted his head and whined in protest.

Pausing, Emily-Ann glanced back at the dog. "We could let him inside for a little while, couldn't we?"

"Are you kidding? He's a cur—a working dog. He's not supposed to be in the house. Doc would have a fit."

"I seriously doubt Chandler would throw a fit. Of all the Hollister brothers, he has the softest heart."

"You say that like you're sure."

She beamed a knowing smile at him. "I should be sure. I've known them since I was in third grade."

And that was a heck of a lot longer than Taggart had been acquainted with the Hollisters. Which made it no surprise that Maureen made no bones about wanting Emily-Ann to be happy and treated with respect. Taggart got the impression that Maureen believed his intentions toward Emily-Ann were honorable and he'd not said anything to make her believe otherwise. So now he could label himself a big hypocrite along with being a coward, he thought grimly.

Caving in to Emily-Ann and the dog, he said,

"Okay. Come on, King. I guess you can be a house dog for a little while."

The three of them entered the house and Taggart promptly excused himself. "I'd better go wash up before we eat," he told her.

"Take your time. I'll get things ready for our supper."

Short minutes later, when he entered the kitchen, he noticed Emily-Ann had set the table with paper plates. As she filled iced glasses with sweet tea, he sniffed the air with appreciation.

"Mmm. How did you know I'd been craving pizza?"

She placed the pitcher on the table. "You talk in your sleep."

Laughing, he walked over to the table and pulled out her chair. "Since when have I ever been asleep while we're in bed together?"

A pink blush stole over her cheeks and he was amazed that the intimate part of their relationship still had that much effect on her.

"Good point," she said with a chuckle.

After she was seated, he made himself comfortable in the chair angled to her right elbow. Emily-Ann promptly opened the lid on the pizza box and offered it to him.

"You must have had last-minute work to keep you late," she said. "I was beginning to think there was an emergency going on."

He placed two wedges of pizza on his plate, while marveling how the day had ended up pulling every ounce of energy from his body. Which didn't make sense. Most of the day he'd spent in the saddle, riding with Maureen, and the rest had been spent at the ranch yard sorting steers to be shipped to Red Bluff.

"No. Nothing like that. I was just running behind on everything that needed to get done. Maureen and I rode most of the morning and part of the afternoon—checking on cows."

She looked faintly surprised, but not nearly as surprised as Taggart had felt this morning when Maureen had approached him with her wishes.

"Oh. Did Gil go with you? I remember you saying he'd been going out every day, working with Maureen."

"No. Gil had to make a trip to Phoenix today."

She cast him a curious glance as she helped herself to the pizza. "I'll bet Gil has been looking into Joel's death. Did Maureen mention anything about it?"

He'd promised Maureen he wouldn't mention that the two of them had ridden to water pump number nine. And he would keep that promise. But he didn't want to lie to Emily-Ann, either. "Only in passing. She's aware that her sons have been investigating the matter. I get the impression she has her own ideas about Joel's death. I can see that Maureen isn't a vindictive person, but if it was ever revealed that Joel was murdered, she'd damn well want justice served."

"And who could blame her for that? Losing Joel was like sticking a knife in the heart of the family."

Taggart didn't make a reply to that and as long seconds ticked by without her saying more, he was relieved that she'd decided to drop the gloomy subject.

"You look exceptionally pretty tonight. That dress is nice." The green-and-white fabric formed a ruffle that fell just off her creamy shoulders. The top part of her hair was wound into a bun, while the rest hung loose against her back.

"Thanks. Actually it's a gift from Camille. She loves to buy me things even though I tell her not to." She looked at him with sad acceptance. "She tells me that she and Matthew are going to be leaving for Red Bluff next week. It'll probably be ages before I see her again."

"Maybe not. Matthew has TooTall to keep things going while he's away. They'll probably come in for a holiday or special occasion."

The smile she gave him was wan at best. "I hope so. Anyway, I can tell when we talk that she's missing the diner and her friends at Dragoon. Maybe they'll make the trip back up here for Sam and Gabby's wedding. That's going to be a very special occasion. Isabelle tells me they're going to throw a

big shindig on the Bar X and invite the whole coun-
tryside."

His sigh was heavy. "I'm not surprised. Weddings
seem to be important functions around here."

She looked at him as though she wanted to say
something, then quickly changed her mind. Was she
thinking it was about time she had a wedding of
her own?

*Don't be stupid, Taggart. Emily-Ann hasn't known
you long enough to fall in love with you, much less
decide she wants to be your wife.*

Maybe not, Taggart thought, as he fought against
the voice inside him. But when she held him, kissed
him, he felt as though she was pouring her heart out
to him. And he'd been just greedy enough to take it.
Or maybe he'd been misinterpreting all those sighs
and kisses and words of desire whispered in his ear.
A woman could enjoy sex without having her heart
involved. Could be she was beginning to think Taggart was a dead-end street and she wanted to travel
down a bigger and better avenue. One where she
could find a man more than willing to marry her.

Finally she said, "Weddings are very important—
to some people."

He didn't know what to say to that and after a
moment they both fell silent until she pushed back
her plate.

"One piece is all I can eat," she said. "You can
save the rest of it for your supper tomorrow night."

He'd never known Emily-Ann to be a finicky eater. "Are you feeling ill?"

"No." She smiled at him as though to prove it. "I'm fine. I just had a very busy day. I had to try to take a test between waiting on customers this morning. It was chaotic. I only hope I passed."

"I had a surprise this morning," he told her. "I got a message from my sister saying that Dad had been bugging her for money. He's threatening to come out here to Arizona."

Her brows lifted. "Threatening? That's a strange word to use in connection with your father."

"Well, if you knew him, you'd understand why I worded it in that way. He causes trouble wherever he goes. And he doesn't ask, he demands. I don't want to have to deal with him, Emily-Ann. And I certainly don't want the Hollisters to meet him."

She reached across the table and smoothed her fingertips over the fresh scar where he'd been bitten by the stallion.

"I wouldn't worry. I'm betting he doesn't have the money to make the trip out here. But he wants you to think he'll show up so that you'll send money to him. Just to make sure he stays away."

"You're probably right. And I can't be worrying about him now. I just don't want him harassing my sister."

She rose from the table and crossed the room to where the coffee machine sat at the end of the cabinet counter. As she began to gather the makings, she said, "Sounds like she's the one who needs to make the trip out here. A one-way trip."

"I've considered the idea of asking her to move here. But I need to get some things…settled before I do."

After she flipped the switch and the coffee began to brew, she walked back over to the table and rested her hands on the back of his shoulders. "What kind of things settled? Your job is secure. And you have a nice home here. You don't have anything else to settle—unless you're talking about your finances."

It suddenly dawned on Taggart that sometime during the past month they'd quit talking like people who were simply dating and started conversing like a man and wife. He couldn't rationalize how or why that had happened. Except that somewhere along the way he'd made a huge mistake. He'd slowly and surely allowed himself to get too close to Emily-Ann.

"I'm not concerned about that." He tilted his head around so that he could look up at her. "When the coffee finishes, I'd like to go to the living room. I need to talk to you about something."

Deep down, Emily-Ann had always known that sooner or later, she'd get the old "we need to talk" from Taggart. Yet she'd thought, or maybe she'd been hoping more than thinking, that she wouldn't hear those final words from him for a long, long while.

And why not? Everything had been going so great between them. If all the passion he'd showered on her this past month had been an act, then he deserved an award for the performance. But passion wasn't love, she realized. And love was the binder that held two people together. Not a set of sweaty sheets.

Emily-Ann carried a tray with their coffee and a saucer of Reeva's homemade cookies into the living room and after setting it on the coffee table, she eased down next to Taggart.

He looked unusually tired this evening and she wondered if spending most of the day with Maureen had stressed him out. Not that the woman was difficult to get along with. On the contrary, she was a joy to be around. But she and Blake were Taggart's bosses. He might've been feeling like he was under a microscope. *Anyway, what did any of that matter now?* she glumly asked herself.

Getting right to the point, she asked, "So what did you want to talk to me about?"

He reached for one of the coffees and took a long sip before he spoke. "I've been doing a lot of thinking about you and me. We've been spending a great deal of time together—both of us driving back and forth from here to Wickenburg. Which is hardly a short distance."

"I haven't minded." Her palms were so sweaty she had to wipe them on a napkin from the tray before she could pick up her coffee cup.

"I don't feel good about it, Emily-Ann. I worry about you driving in the dark on these lonely dirt roads. It isn't safe."

She didn't know where he was going with this. "I guess you're thinking about your late wife now."

He looked at her with something like surprise and then the expression turned to a glower. "No. I'm not thinking about her. I'm thinking about *you*—being safe."

"Oh. But surely you're not thinking you'll do all the driving to my place."

"No. I'm not. I'm young and healthy, but I don't think I could hold up to that pace and work, too."

Over the rim of her cup, she studied his face and tried to interpret the expressions she saw in his eyes and on his lips. He looked frustrated and lost and most of all weary. But from what? Was she doing this to him?

"Okay. So I guess this means you want us to slow down. To just see each other once in a while. Is that what you're trying to tell me?"

He looked at her and frowned. "Hell, no. What I'm trying to tell you is that I want you to move in with me."

Emily-Ann had never been so stunned in her life. For the past fifteen minutes she'd resigned herself to the fact that he wanted to end things. Instead, he was asking her to move in!

She must have stared at him far longer than she

thought because he finally scooted to the edge of the cushion and squared around to face her.

"Well? You're not saying anything. What do you think?"

"I wasn't expecting this from you." Dazed, she rose and walked across the room to where the main door had been left open to allow the cool night air to sift through an old-fashioned screen door. "If you want me to be completely honest, I don't like it."

Her throat was so thick she was surprised he'd heard the choked words. But he must have because he was suddenly standing directly behind her and so close that she could feel the heat radiating from his body.

"Why don't you like it?"

How could she begin to answer his question when she couldn't even explain the reasons to herself? She only knew that if she moved in with Taggart, she'd be giving up everything she'd ever wanted for herself.

"I—just don't think it's a good idea," she whispered, as the reality of his feelings were suddenly becoming quite clear to her.

His hands came down on her shoulders and for a second the emptiness inside of her wanted to turn and grab hold of him.

"You have something against a man and a woman living together—is that it?"

"No. It's probably the right choice for some people. Just not for me."

Awkward moments of silence began to tick away as she held her breath and waited for his response. Yet even as she clung to the tiniest hope that he'd say something—anything about loving her, she knew deep down that he was never going to have those kinds of feelings for her.

"I thought you liked being with me," he reasoned. "And I definitely want to be with you. I thought us living together here on the ranch was a good solution."

A solution to what? she wanted to ask. His urge to have sex whenever he wanted? Maybe that was enough for him, but not for her.

Her throat aching, she whispered, "Moving in with a guy has never been what I've planned for myself, Tag."

He tightened his hold on her shoulders. "A person can change their plans."

"Yes, and I can see I'm definitely going to have to change mine."

"What does that mean?" he asked.

Summoning up more strength than she ever dreamed she possessed, she turned to face him and then nearly wilted as her gaze met his. Confusion and disappointment swirled in the brown depths of his eyes.

She said, "It means that I think it would be best if we didn't see each other anymore."

He visibly flinched and she realized she'd surprised him. No doubt he'd seen her as too besotted with him to walk away. Well, she *was* besotted with the man, she thought sickly. More than that. She was in love with him. But no way would she ever admit that to him now. No, at least this way she could walk away with some shred of pride in herself.

"Are you serious?"

"Never more so," she said flatly. "You've made your feelings clear, Tag. And frankly, we're not on the same page."

A scowl caused his brows to form one dark line. "Am I supposed to understand that?"

Sighing, she reached up and gently touched her fingers to his dear face. For days after he'd given her the flowers, she gazed at them and allowed herself to believe they might have a real future together as man and wife—the whole family shebang. What a gullible idiot she'd been.

"No. I don't expect you to understand, Tag. And I'm sorry that you feel slighted. It's all my fault, really. When we first met, you made your feelings clear about love and marriage. I should've run from you then. But I didn't. So here we are at a dead end. That's all."

She hadn't thought it was possible for his frown to go any deeper but somehow it did. Taut lines ran from the corners of his mouth and eyes and furrowed his brow. He looked like a man in physical pain, but she knew that wasn't the case. Not over losing her.

A man had to love beforehand to experience that kind of loss.

"Love and marriage? Don't you think you're rushing things?"

His disbelief verged on the comical and the reality that he considered love and marriage to her a joke was all it took to have her backing away from him.

"Get this straight, Tag, I'm not asking anything from you. Now or ever! So relax. Go have yourself a good laugh."

She stalked over to the end table where she'd left her handbag when she'd arrived earlier this evening. After shouldering the leather strap, she walked back to the door with King trotting right on her heels.

"This is your way of solving things?" he asked, his voice incredulous.

She struggled to keep her lips from quivering. "There's nothing to solve. I'm glad for the time we spent together, but all good things come to an end. We both know that. But if you ever decide you want a cup of coffee and a pastry, you know how to find Conchita's."

She pushed past him and out the door. In spite of the pain ripping her heart and the tears swimming in her eyes, she put one foot in front of the other until she was down the porch and out to her car.

When she opened the door to climb in, she realized King had followed her and the sight of the whining dog was enough to cause a sob to slip past her lips.

Kneeling down to him, she cradled his face with both hands. "King, you can't come with me. You have to stay here on the ranch and hunt cows in the brush. That's your job. Tag will take care of you and someday—maybe—I'll see you again."

She dropped a kiss on top of the dog's head, then quickly climbed in the car and drove away. It wasn't until she was a quarter mile away from the house that she noticed King was chasing after her.

Blocking the dog and Taggart from her mind, she pressed down on the accelerator and headed the car onto the main road that would take her back to Wick-enburg. Where she belonged.

Taggart stood on the porch and stared into the darkness where Emily-Ann's taillights had disappeared only minutes before.

What in hell had just happened? How could she just leave like that without giving him a chance to explain and reason with her?

Forget the past. Move forward. Hell! That's exactly what he'd been trying to do when he'd asked Emily-Ann to move in with him. But she'd taken the invitation as an insult. Maureen's theory on life was probably good for her, but it hadn't work for Taggart, he thought glumly.

He muttered a curse, then stuck two fingers in his mouth and let out a loud whistle.

"King! Come here, you damned traitor! There's no use chasing after a woman who doesn't want us!"

A couple of long minutes passed before the dog finally emerged from the dark lane and trotted up to the house.

As King approached the porch, Taggart started to give him a harsh scolding, but that plan was waylaid the minute the dog sat down next to him and let out a pathetic whine.

"Okay, boy," Taggart said, as he bent to pat the dog's head. "You're not in trouble. You'll just have to forget about her. That's what I'm going to do."

He turned and started back into the house and King determinedly trotted behind him. When they reached the screen door, Taggart hesitated for only a moment before he allowed the dog to follow him into the house.

The tray of coffee and cookies that Emily-Ann had carried to the living room were still on the coffee table. He picked it up and carried it to the kitchen where their meal of pizza was still scattered over the table and nearby cabinet counter.

Taggart began to clear away the mess, while wishing he could clear away the agony and confusion he was feeling.

Today, for the first time in years, he'd decided it was time to try to tear down the walls he'd built around his heart. Not just because Maureen had suggested he move on from the past, but because he felt like things between him and Emily-Ann had reached a point where snatching pieces of time here and there to be together was no longer enough. He'd thought having her move in would be the next logical step. Then he'd have plenty of time to get used to the idea of having her in his life for the long haul. He'd have a chance to decide if he really wanted to commit that much of himself to her.

And what the hell was Emily-Ann supposed to do while you sat around trying to make up your mind, Taggart? She deserves more than a trial run from you and you know it. So if that's all you can give her, then you got exactly what you deserve—a swift goodbye.

Damn. Damn. Taggart silently cursed as he tried to shut out the condemning voice in his head. Didn't he have a reason to be cautious? Didn't he have a right to think things through before he handed another woman his heart?

Yes, he did. But that didn't mean he had the right to take her to bed and expect that to be all she needed or wanted, he thought miserably.

Jamming the leftover pizza back into its box, he shoved it into the refrigerator, then got out his phone and punched his sister's number.

He was sinking into a chair at the table when she finally answered.

"Hi, Tag. How's my sweet brother?"

Sweet? Right now he felt as bitter as a green persimmon. "I'm fine," he lied, while wondering what he could do to get the clenched knot out of his stomach and the pain in his chest to go away. "I'm just calling to check on you."

There was a moment's pause and then she said, "I'm sorry if my text this morning caused you to worry about me. Everything is okay, Tag, really. I can handle Dad."

"Yeah, by tiptoeing around him like a Gila monster."

She sighed and Taggart could easily picture his sister with her dark hair hanging around her shoulders and her brown eyes full of warmth. Tallulah not only resembled their late mother, but she also possessed her soft heart. That was one of the reasons he didn't want her to have to deal with Buck O'Brien. She wasn't emotionally strong enough. Especially now that she and Trent had gotten divorced.

"He's not that bad—yet. But I'm thinking he's gotten into some kind of trouble that he doesn't want me to find out about."

Taggart gripped the phone, while wondering how much more his aching head could handle tonight. "What kind of trouble?" he dared to ask.

"I don't know anything for sure. It's just a hunch that he might be involved with some nasty loan sharks and they're breathing down his neck to be repaid. He seems more desperate than usual."

He groaned out loud. "That's just dandy. What's the old man going to do next, huh?"

"Who knows? Just be glad you're out there in Arizona, far away from the man, Tag."

He'd thought leaving the Flying W, and the demanding new owners, along with his shiftless father, would make his life free of stress and worry. Now he realized how ridiculous that sort of thinking had been. This rip between him and Emily-Ann was like nothing he'd ever endured. But he couldn't let himself think about her now. If he did, he might just break down and spill the whole pitiful mess to his sister.

"That's another reason I'm calling, sis. I've been doing some thinking. About you."

A teasing chuckle sounded in his ear. "Missing me already?"

"Sure I am. You're the only family I have."

There was a moment of silence and then he caught the soft sound of her sigh.

"You're the only family I have, too, Tag."

"That makes what I'm about to propose make even more sense," he told her. "I'd like for you to move out here, Tally."

"To Arizona? And live with you?" She sounded flabbergasted

"Yes, to Arizona. And yes, live with me for a

while. Until you get settled and then I figure you'd like to get a place of your own nearby."

"I'd definitely want that. Otherwise, we'd be trying to tear each other's hair out."

"You mean like we did when we were kids?"

"Exactly."

He could hear a smile in her voice, but the sound wasn't enough to lift the corners of his mouth. He felt like every cell in his body was frozen with pain and shock. Would this awful emptiness go away by tomorrow? Or would he have to wait a week or even months before he began to feel like a human being again?

"I'm serious, Tally."

"I understand that you're serious, Tag. But all my friends are here. So is my job at the real estate office. And—"

"You can get a better job here. That damned boss of yours is just using you. He makes bucket loads of money and pays you like you're the janitor instead of a secretary. He's a jerk and you're putting up with it."

A long stretch of silence passed before she finally spoke. "What in the world is wrong with you, brother? You sound like you're ready to coldcock somebody. Has something happened?"

Yes, something has happened, he thought. His whole world had just stopped spinning and no matter how hard he tried, he couldn't see any sort of happiness in his future.

"No," he said sharply. "Everything here is great."

"You could've fooled me. I'm afraid to hear what you'd sound like if something bad really had happened. Just proves to me that I'd rather stay here and be used by Mr. Graves than be growled at by my bearish brother."

Closing his eyes, he raked a hand through his tumbled hair. If Emily-Ann hadn't walked out on him, he would've already had her in bed by now. At this very moment she would've been kissing him, loving him in a way that no woman had ever loved him.

Love. Love. He never wanted to hear the word or have it enter his mind ever again, he thought bitterly. He didn't want to think that he'd just lost his one and only chance to know what real love actually felt like.

"I'm sorry, Tally. It's been a long, stressful day. I didn't mean to sound sharp. You're my favorite sis, you know."

She laughed then. "I'm your *only* sis. Remember?"

"Yeah, I remember. So will you seriously consider my invitation?"

There was another long pause and she finally said, "Yes. I will think deep and hard about it, Tag."

They talked a minute more and then Taggart finally ended the call and left the kitchen. When he entered the living room, he saw King pawing at the screen door.

The sight was like a knife slicing right through him and for the first time in years he was finding it hard to hold his emotions together. "Okay, so you want out. Now that Emily-Ann isn't here you don't like it inside. Well, just go." He opened the screen door and King shot onto the porch and down the steps like the devil was following him. "Go on back to Doc," he called after the yellow cur. "That's where you belong. And don't come back thinking she'll be here. She's gone."

And she won't be coming back.

The heavy weight of that reality settled on Taggart's shoulders as he shut the door and bolted it.

Chapter Twelve

"Emily-Ann, is that you?"

About to step out of the glass foyer and onto the wide sidewalk, Emily-Ann turned to see Camille bearing down on her.

Oh Lord, Camille was the last person she'd expected to run into here at the medical clinic. What was she going to tell her? That she had to visit the doctor because she couldn't eat? Couldn't stop crying?

Biting back a helpless groan, she squared her shoulders and waited for Camille to catch up to her.

"Camille, what are you doing here? Are you having a problem with the baby?"

Her friend quickly dismissed the question with a wave of her hand. "We're in fine shape. Matthew wanted me to have an extra checkup before we travel home," she explained, then laughed. "I think he's worried I'll go into labor while he's driving. He'll be pulling a trailer load of steers back with us and he doesn't think he can handle them and me having a baby at the same time."

Emily-Ann tried to laugh, but couldn't summon up anything that resembled a sound of amusement. She'd left the doctor's office in shock and the fog in her brain was still muddling her senses.

Camille peered closely at Emily-Ann. "What are you doing here at the clinic? Have you been sick or just having a yearly checkup?"

"Neither. I—uh, nothing serious. I've just been feeling a bit off, that's all." Deciding it would be pointless to hide the news from her closest friend, she grabbed Camille by the arm and urged her through the sliding glass doors. Once they were outside, she pointed down the sidewalk to a concrete bench shaded by the overhang of the building. "Do you have time to sit a minute?"

"Are you kidding? I'm not going anywhere until you tell me why you look like you've stuck your face in a bowl of flour."

They walked down to the bench and after both of them were comfortably seated, Camille leveled an anxious look at her.

"Okay, out with it," she demanded. "You were lying to me a minute ago. Something is seriously wrong with you."

"Something is wrong all right," Emily-Ann ruefully agreed. "With my head. I'm a stupid woman, Camille. There's no better way to explain the reason I had to visit the doctor."

Camille rolled her eyes. "You can't fix stupid at this clinic, Emily-Ann."

She groaned. "You're right. The doctor can't fix it. But he can certainly diagnose it!"

Camille must've decided that Emily-Ann's health wasn't in dire jeopardy because a perceptive grin suddenly appeared on her face. "Uh-huh. So what have you done? Spent too much money on something you didn't need and now you're getting ulcers worrying about it?"

The sound that burst past Emily-Ann's lips was something between a sob and a hysterical laugh. "How could I do that when I barely have enough to pay bills?"

Camille's expression softened as she reached over and gently rubbed the top of Emily-Ann's hand. "I'm sorry. I'm only teasing. I can see you're upset. Tell me what's going on with your health. Did the doctor give you a prescription?"

Emily-Ann pulled a small square of paper from her purse and thrust it at her friend. "Only this. I can buy them off the shelf."

Camille read the scribbled words, which promptly caused her mouth to fall open and her shocked gaze to fly up to Emily-Ann's face. "Prenatal vitamins! You're pregnant?"

Nodding, Emily-Ann fought at the tears scalding the back of her eyes. "Dr. Revere believes I'm about a month along. I don't know how it happened, Camille."

In spite of Emily-Ann's obvious distress, Camille laughed. "Of course you know how it happened. Every woman does."

Emily-Ann tried to clear the gravelly lump that had formed in her throat. "Well, yes, that part of it I know. I got too close to a long tall Texan! Obviously he was more potent than the pill I'm taking! That's my theory on the matter. The doctor seems to think the pregnancy occurred because I had a cold for a few days and that can sometimes affect the strength of the pill."

Her eyes twinkling with delight, Emily-Ann said, "When you two met at the party, I was fairly certain you and Tag were going to hit it off."

"Hit it off!" Emily-Ann practically shouted. "We've done more than that. We've created a baby!"

Camille's smile spread wider. "This is wonderful, Emily-Ann! Our children will practically be the same age—only a few months difference. They might both turn out to be redheads and grow up to be great friends, like us."

Camille made it sound like Emily-Ann had just been handed the best news a woman could ever receive. And it suddenly dawned on her that her friend was so very right. A child was a blessed gift. Plus, she'd always dreamed of having children. She had to feel happy about the pregnancy, even if it was an unexpected shock.

"That part would be nice," Emily-Ann agreed. "I only wish—oh, Camille, I don't want this baby to grow up without a father. I don't want my child to ever have to know that he or she wasn't important enough to deserve a full-time father."

Frowning, Camille squeezed her hands. "I don't understand. Don't you think Tag will be happy about the baby? I surely do. He has family man written all over him."

"Hah! Not a family with me, Camille." Shaking her head, she pulled a tissue from her handbag and dabbed it at her teary eyes. "I'm sorry. You couldn't know that Tag and I ended things a week ago. I haven't seen or talked with him since I was out at his house. But now—well, I'm going to have to face him with this new development. And I'm not looking forward to it."

Camille was silent for a thoughtful moment and then she said, "I wasn't aware that anything had happened between you two. Tag must not have mentioned it to Matthew or my brothers. But that's hardly a surprise. What little I've been around him, he doesn't do much talking about himself." She turned a questioning look at Emily-Ann: "So what happened? He's found someone else? Or he's tired of dating?"

Emily-Ann glanced around at the people going to and from the medical building to the large parking lot. This wasn't exactly the ideal place to be discussing something so private, but no one seemed to be paying the two women any mind. Most of them were probably dealing with their own troubles, she thought glumly.

She pushed out a heavy breath. "Nothing like that. Tag asked me to move in with him. And I—obviously, I refused."

"Oh. Move in," Camille murmured. "I see."

Bitter gall was spreading from her chest to the back of her throat, practically choking her. "No. I doubt you understand. So go ahead and tell me I'm an idiot for not grabbing what he offered. And maybe I am the biggest one to ever walk the earth—I don't know. But I am sure about one thing—I'm not going to be like my mother. I'm not going to live my life with a man who doesn't love me."

"Oh, Emily-Ann, this is—I don't know what to say. Except that if Tag wanted you to move in with him that certainly doesn't sound like a man who's tired of you. Or that he doesn't want to be involved."

Bending her head, Emily-Ann muttered, "You don't understand, Camille. He wants the convenience. It's nothing about having deep feelings for me. All the time we were together, he didn't say anything about caring for me—really caring. And then last week before I left, I finally got so angry I brought up the words *love* and *marriage*."

"And?"

"He looked like I'd thrown cold water in his face." Lifting her head, she shook it with grim determination. "No. I made the mistake of falling into the same trap my mother did. She believed she'd found love when actually all she'd been was a sex partner."

"Emily-Ann, I'm having a hard time believing that! Tag doesn't come off as that kind to me. How do you think he's going to react when he hears about the baby?"

Emily-Ann lifted her gaze to the cloudless sky. "I'm clueless there. I'm guessing he's not going to be a bit pleased. I imagine he'll be thinking I want to hook him into marriage." Her lips clamped tightly together, she looked at Camille. "Well, he's in for a surprise. I'd rather walk down the aisle with a jackass!"

Camille was clearly disappointed. "Why are you thinking like this?"

"I'll tell you why. All her life, my mother got nothing but crumbs from my biological father and then from the man she finally married. I'm not going to settle for crumbs, Camille."

"Damn it, Emily-Ann, you aren't your mother!"

"That's right. And I don't ever intend to be." Rising to her feet, she grabbed up her handbag. "I need to go. I took the afternoon off work to visit the doctor and now I have online classes scheduled. I can't afford to miss them."

Reaching down, she gave Camille a hand up from the bench.

Once she was on her feet, Camille said, "I think Matthew is planning on leaving for Red Bluff Sunday morning. Hopefully I can see you again before we go." She smacked a kiss on Emily-Ann's cheek. "I love you. Don't worry. You're going to have a baby and that's all that really matters."

Emily-Ann gave her a wobbly smile. "You're right. This little life I'm carrying means everything to me. And I'm not the only woman in the world who can be a good single mom."

"Now, you're talking." She gave Emily-Ann a parting hug. "Chin up. Everything is going to be fine."

Emily-Ann gave her friend a grateful squeeze, then hurried away before she could see the tears in her eyes.

"You don't have anything planned for tomorrow evening, do you?"

From his seat in the cushy leather armchair, Taggart glanced across Blake's office to where the man sat behind his desk, signing off on purchases for grain and fencing supplies.

After a long workday in the saddle, Taggart had

received a brief text from the man asking him to stop by the office to discuss plans for cutting the irrigated hay meadows. If the grass was ready, haying usually began the next month. But so far the two men had talked about everything but the hay. "Not unless you count doing my laundry and fixing myself something to eat."

"I can't help you with the laundry, but forget the cooking. Reeva will take care of that chore. I realize tomorrow night is Saturday night, but Mom has her heart set on you having dinner with us. It's a good-bye thing for Matthew and Camille."

Taggart wasn't decent company for anyone, but to make Maureen happy and to show Matthew his appreciation for all the support the man had given him these past six weeks, he supposed he could fake it and smile his way through the evening.

"I'll be glad to show up. Actually, I need to present Matthew with some kind of award for all the patience he's shown me since I arrived. He not only taught me lots of things about the ranch, but he also made me feel at home. I'm going to miss him."

"We're all going to miss him. And Camille—well, just when we get her back here on the ranch for a little while, she's leaving again." Leaning back in his chair, he linked his hands at the back of his neck and let out a long sigh. "But this time is different. She's happy and in love. And we don't worry about her anymore, because we know Matthew will take good care of her."

Take good care of her. There'd been times when Emily-Ann had been lying next to him that he'd wanted to hold her tight and promise he'd always take care of her, that he'd always be there for her no matter what the future held. But each time the promises had lodged in his throat. Because each time he'd realized no man can stop fate from stepping in and wiping away the things he loved the most.

Love. That awful night Emily-Ann had left his house, he'd vowed to never let the word enter his mind. But these past few days his mind had gone rogue on him. All it seemed to want to think about was love and how he'd lost his chance at having it, holding it and cherishing it.

Shaking away the bitter thoughts, Taggart focused his attention back to the present. "Yes, Matthew is a good man. He'll make a fine father, too."

Blake gathered the stack of papers he'd just signed and placed them on the corner of his desk before he glanced over at Taggart. "You know, you ought to invite Emily-Ann out to have dinner with us. She'll be wanting to see Camille before she leaves."

Blake might as well have thrown a bucket of ice on him, Taggart thought. He was so frozen by the man's suggestion that for a moment he couldn't speak. Finally, he managed to say, "I don't think that's a good idea. Uh—besides, it's your mother's party. It's her place to do the inviting."

And if Emily-Ann was going to be there, he didn't think he could bear it, Taggart thought.

Blake frowned at him. "Why wouldn't it be a good idea? I thought you and Emily-Ann were getting along great."

Too restless to remain in the armchair, Taggart got up and poured himself a cup of hours-old coffee and added several spoons of sugar. "We were. But things have changed. We're not seeing each other anymore."

A long stretch of silence passed before Blake finally said, "Oh. I'm sorry to hear that. I thought—"

Blake went silent again and Taggart slanted a curious glance in his direction. "You thought what?"

Leveling a shrewd look at him, Blake answered, "That you two might actually be getting serious about each other."

The pain in Taggart's chest was so unbearable he swallowed several gulps of the awful coffee before he could speak. "I don't know why you'd come up with that idea. I'm not a serious kind of guy. Not where women are concerned. Emily-Ann figured that out for herself. And—that's probably all for the best. No ties or broken hearts. You know what I mean."

His expression solemn, Blake continued to study him. "Yeah. I know what you're saying. You've already lost a woman you loved. You don't want to go through it again."

Taggart's eyes narrowed. "You've been talking to your mother."

"No. Why? Have you?"

There was no way Taggart was going to break his promise to Maureen and tell Blake, or anyone for that matter, that the two of them had ridden to water pump number nine. Nor was he going to tell him the personal things they'd talked about.

"Uh—no. I just thought—well, women kind of have an intuition about men—and she might have voiced her thoughts about me to you."

"No. But I read your background check before we ever hired you. I just never mentioned you're a widower because there was no point in bringing the matter up."

Taggart frowned. "But you think there's a point now?"

"I do. Because I hate to see you make a big mistake. One you might regret for the rest of your life."

Taggart swigged down the last of the coffee and tossed the foam cup into a trash basket next to the small refreshment table. "If you're talking about Emily-Ann, that's over. She wants more than I can give her."

"Guess you're talking about love and marriage now. Well, why shouldn't she want that for herself? Why should she settle for anything less?"

Moving in with a guy has never been what I've planned for myself, Tag.

Emily-Ann's words circled his weary brain, just as they had a thousand times since she'd walked out the door several nights ago. He'd hurt her terribly. He could see that now. But how did he go about trying to repair the damage? Would she even let him try?

With a heavy sigh, Taggart sank back into the armchair and dropped his head into his hands. "There's no use in me trying to act like I'm a cool piece of steel, Blake. I've been miserable without Emily-Ann. I guess—I didn't realize how much she'd come to mean to me until I—until she was gone." Lifting his head, he cast Blake a wry look. "That's the way it is with a fool, isn't it? He never appreciates what he has until he loses it."

Shaking his head, Blake said, "You're not a fool, you're just a little scared like every other man who's ever loved a woman. You've already learned the hard way that standing at the altar and saying your vows doesn't mean you get a guarantee with the marriage license. Regrettably, our mother learned the same thing. You think my brothers and I weren't afraid to take wives and have children? We all wanted to run like chickens. But we all had sense enough to know that living alone and miserable wasn't a good alternative."

Dear God, he'd been alone for a long time and during those empty years he'd believed that was the answer, the alternative to having his heart torn apart.

But Emily-Ann had shown him that living behind a guarded wall was not really living at all.

"I just wonder if Emily-Ann might give me a second chance."

Smiling now, Blake picked up the purchase orders, then switched off the banker's lamp on his desk. "I'll have Mom invite her. In the meantime, you be thinking about what you're going to say to her. Something meaningful and persuasive."

"You mean like I'm a heel and a jerk?"

Blake laughed. "That'll be a start."

Seeing Blake was shutting things down for the night, Taggart rose to his feet. "I thought we were going to discuss the hay meadows?"

He grabbed his Stetson from a hall tree and levered it on his head. "Oh that. We'll go over the hay situation later on."

Taggart shot him a suspicious look. "Damn it, Blake, did you call me in here to talk about Emily-Ann?"

Blake let loose a guilty laugh. "Look, Tag, you might as well get used to us poking into your private life. You're family now and we want everyone in our family to be happy."

Happy? Was there a chance that he could still find happiness with Emily-Ann? He could only hope.

The next evening in the den of the Three Rivers Ranch house, Emily-Ann sat in an armchair with a dessert plate filled with strawberry torte carefully balanced on her knees. Normally she loved the sweet dish, but tonight she'd only managed three bites before her jangled nerves made it nearly impossible to swallow anything past her tight throat.

Camille must have noticed that she was merely pushing the dessert around the plate rather than eating it, because she suddenly spoke up.

"Emily-Ann, would you like for Jazelle to fetch you a different dessert? You've hardly touched the one you have. You might like the pecan pie better."

Emily-Ann glanced over to a leather love seat, where her friend was cuddled comfortably next to her husband's side.

"No!" she blurted out, while thinking she'd never touch another piece of pecan pie as long as she lived. After sharing one with Taggart, it would never taste the same. "I—uh—this is fine. I ate so much for dinner that I really don't have room for dessert."

Maureen walked up on the group just in time to hear Emily-Ann's excuse for her lack of appetite. Now the woman ran a keen gaze over Emily-Ann's face.

"You ate like a bird," Maureen insisted. "And you look peaked, honey. Are you feeling okay?"

She shouldn't have worn this damned yellow dress, Emily-Ann thought. It made her appear even more washed out than she already looked.

"Sure, I'm feeling wonderful." Between bouts of

nausea and having every nerve in her body clenched in a viselike grip, she felt just dandy, she thought sickly. "And dinner was delicious. I'm just feeling a little blue at the idea of telling Camille goodbye."

"You can always come visit us," Matthew spoke up. "We'd be glad to have you."

"That's very nice of you, Matthew. Maybe after your baby gets here I can drive down for a visit. But only for a very quick one. You two are going to have your hands full without added company."

"Well, once baby Matthew gets here, she's definitely going to have to put up with her mother and her sister for a few days," Maureen said teasingly. "But we already have it in mind to shoo Camille off to the diner and keep the baby all to ourselves."

"Hah!" Camille laughed. "Baby Matthew. Who says?"

"TooTall," Matthew answered as if that guaranteed the gender of the baby would be male.

While the three of them continued to discuss the baby and TooTall's prediction, Emily-Ann couldn't help but notice how Matthew had his arm around his wife's shoulders and how the man kept darting loving glances at her. How would that feel, she wondered?

The question had her directing a furtive gaze across the room where Taggart, Holt and Chandler were standing near a wet bar, seemingly in deep conversation.

Thankfully at dinner, Maureen had seated Emily-

Ann several chairs on down the table from Taggart, which had made it much easier to avoid looking in his direction. And since then, she'd not once allowed her gaze to land on his handsome face. She couldn't bear it. Just being in the same room with him made her feel sick and stupid and humiliated.

So far tonight, she'd avoided facing him head-on, but at some point before the evening ended she was going to have to speak with him about the baby. Was he going to be angry? Was he going to accuse her of using her body to set a snare for him? Even if he didn't react quite that harshly, he was still going to throw some hard questions at her and how was she going to answer them?

Oh God, the mere thought of standing in front of him, telling him he was going to have a child, was enough to cause clammy sweat to pop out on her forehead and the base of her throat.

Certain if she didn't get some fresh air, she was going to throw up in front of everyone, Emily-Ann jumped up from the couch. "Please excuse me," she said, darting a frantic glance at Camille. "I, uh, need to step out for a moment."

As she hurried toward the French doors that led out to the patio, she noticed Camille starting to rise to her feet, but Maureen said something that caused her daughter to immediately sink back down on the love seat.

Thank God, Emily-Ann thought, as much as she

loved Camille, her frayed nerves weren't ready for a pep talk or sermon from her dear friend.

She didn't realize just how far she'd walked until she found herself standing by the cottonwood where she'd found Taggart the night of the party. Had she unconsciously sought out the spot, or was fate simply playing cruel tricks on her? It didn't matter, she decided. Nothing mattered now, except the child growing inside her. His child.

She was leaning against the trunk of the tree, allowing the cool air to wash over her when she heard a twig snap behind her.

Thinking Camille had probably come out to check on her, she turned with a weary sigh, then promptly gasped at the sight of Taggart walking out of the shadows.

By the time he reached her side, she'd managed to gather herself enough to speak. "What are you doing out here?"

"I could ask you the same thing."

"Getting some fresh air," she said stiffly, then turned her back to him and gazed blindly out toward the ranch yard in the far distance.

He said, "I guess you came to dinner because of Camille."

The familiar sound of his voice was like shards of glass raining over her. "And you're here because of Matthew."

"Yeah. We both had an obligation to show up for our mutual friends."

She heard him take a step closer and the idea that he might actually touch her sent her shredded nerves into chaos.

"You purposely followed me out here," she said in a strained voice. "Why?"

"I've been trying all evening to find a private moment to speak with you. When I saw you running out of the den, I decided to follow."

Had she actually been running? Lord, everyone in the room must be thinking she'd lost her mind. And they wouldn't be far off from the truth. For the past week and a half she'd done nothing but cry and throw up everything she put in her stomach. She'd reached the point where she hardly knew what she was doing or saying.

"Oh. Well, you've solved my problem. Because I've been wondering how I could talk to you—alone."

"Really? You haven't so much as looked at me tonight. I can't imagine you wanting to talk to me," he said. "You left the house more than a week ago and I've not heard a word from you. That doesn't sound like a woman who wants to talk."

Was it possible for a heart to split down the middle and still keep beating, she wondered? Because hers felt as though it was slowly and surely cracking.

"I've not heard a word from you, either. But then

I didn't expect to. You've made your feelings clear and I've accepted that what we had is over."

"Is it?"

Suspicious now, she studied his shadowed face. "I haven't changed my mind about anything, Tag. If that's what you're thinking."

"I don't want you to change your mind," he said flatly.

The pain in her chest was practically wiping out her ability to breathe and she had to turn her back to him as tears began to fill her eyes. "Oh. Well, that's that. So if you don't mind, would you please go back inside and leave me alone? I don't want to—continue this conversation—not tonight."

"Sorry, Emily-Ann, but I'm not going to leave you alone. Not until I say a few things that… I think you ought to hear."

Bending her head, she swallowed hard. "All right. Say them," she whispered.

His hands suddenly settled on her shoulders and all the familiar feelings of his touch poured through her like warm rain.

"I don't know where to start. So I'll just begin by saying I've been a complete jerk—an idiot. And I'm sorry. Terribly sorry."

Hope tried to enter her heart, but she immediately slammed the door on it. His being sorry didn't change the fact he wanted a bed partner rather than a wife.

"What do you have to be sorry about?" she mumbled the question. "Being honest?"

"But I haven't been honest," he admitted, then gently turned her so that she was facing him. "You've turned me into a habitual liar, Emily-Ann. Ever since I met you, I've continued to lie to you and myself. I've been telling myself I didn't love you. That I didn't need you in my life. Not as a wife or the mother of my children. But all along I knew I was lying and yet I was too much of a coward to face up to my real feelings."

She shook her head with disbelief. "Are you trying to say that…you love me?"

"Yes. But I'm butchering it up pretty badly, aren't I?"

A sob burst past her lips and then he was pulling her into his arms, holding her so tight that the side of her face was crushed against his chest.

"I'm hearing it, Tag. But I—"

"I know. You don't believe me. But I promise, Emily-Ann, I'll spend the rest of my life showing you just how much I love you. That is, if you'll let me."

Wedging her hands against his chest, she levered herself away enough to see his face. "I don't understand, Tag. You didn't want strings, or love or marriage. Why now?"

"Ask King. He'll tell you how miserable I've been without you. It only took me a couple of days to realize that my job, my home, my life meant nothing if you weren't with me."

The reality that he really did love her was beginning to set in and the joy that was pouring into her heart was healing the broken cracks she'd felt only minutes before. "And the rest of the days we've been apart?"

"I've been trying to figure out how to get you back—wondering if you could possibly forgive me." Reaching up, he stroked a hand over her hair. "I asked you to move in with me because—I was too afraid to ask you to be my wife. But I'm asking you now, Emily-Ann. Will you marry me?"

His declaration of love had been far more than she'd ever expected to hear from him. Now, he was proposing. It was almost more than she could take in. "Marry you!" she finally whispered. "Are you serious?"

He reached into the front pocket of his jeans and pulled out a velvet ring box. "I went to town yesterday and bought this because I knew you'd be here tonight. Ever since I've been praying you'll accept it."

When he flipped open the lid, Emily-Ann sucked in a sharp breath. The engagement ring was a large square-shaped diamond, flanked by two smaller emeralds and set in filigreed gold. It was far beyond anything Emily-Ann had ever dreamed a man might give her.

"Oh my! Oh, Tag, it's so beautiful! But it's too much," she protested. "A girl like me—"

"A girl like you deserves something beautiful," he finished.

Dazed, Emily-Ann watched him pull the ring from its velvet bed, but when he took her hand to push it onto her finger, she promptly shook her head and pulled back.

"I can't accept it, Tag. Not yet. Not until I tell you something you need to know."

Frowning, he dropped the ring into his shirt pocket. "Okay, what? That you don't love me? Well, I don't care. I'll love you enough for both of us."

She touched a hand to her forehead as her mind whirled with everything that had just happened. "I don't know how to tell you this, except to just come right out with it. You're going to be a father."

It was his turn to look flabbergasted. "A father! Are you saying you're pregnant?"

She nodded, still uncertain how the news of the baby was going to affect him. "About a month or so along. I guess it happened when we—uh—first got together. The doctor said my pill lost some of its strength because I had a cold, but that hardly changes the fact now."

He leaned back his head and let out a joyous shout. "A baby! Our baby!"

Smiling ear to ear, he lifted her off her feet and

whirled her around until she was laughing breath-lessly.

"Are you really pleased, Tag?"

He set her back on her feet, then pulled her into his arms and kissed her for long, long moments. "Pleased? Oh, my darling, I couldn't be any happier."

Fifteen minutes ago, her heart was bursting with pain, now it was overflowing with joy. "I started to tell you when you first walked up. Now I'm so very glad I didn't. I'll always know that you wanted me to be your wife before you learned about the baby. I didn't want you thinking I'd gotten pregnant to snare you."

He pressed his lips to her forehead. "You got pregnant because you gave yourself to me. Because you put your love and trust in me. And I promise you, darling Emily-Ann, that I'll cherish you and our children the rest of my life."

Leaning her head back, she looked at him with starry eyes. "Children? As in plural?"

He chuckled. "You don't think we'll stop with one, do you? We have a long ways to go to catch up with the Hollisters."

Fetching the ring from his pocket, he slipped it onto her finger, then placed a soft, promising kiss upon her lips.

"Let's go tell everyone our happy news," he said.

She reached for his hand and just as they turned to walk back to the house, she began to laugh.

Pausing, Taggart asked, "What now?"

"I caught Camille's bridal bouquet at her and Matthew's wedding and ever since she's been predicting that I'd be getting married soon," Emily-Ann explained. "I'll never hear the end of this. She'll swear that the bouquet brought us together."

Laughing, Taggart tugged her on toward the house. "Come on, I'm going to go thank her for not throwing those flowers to anyone else but you."

Epilogue

On the last Saturday in June, the hot Arizona sun dipped behind a ridge of red, rocky bluff to spread a spectacular sunset of pink and gold over the huge crowd that had gathered at the Bar X to watch Gabby Townsend and Sam Leman exchange their vows of love.

The wedding ceremony was the second one Emily-Ann and Taggart had attended in the past three weeks, the first one being their own. Which had been a simple, yet elegant ceremony the Hollisters had given them at Three Rivers Ranch.

However, this wedding was far different from Emily-Ann and Taggart's. This event could only be described as a whopper of a shindig. People from every corner of Yavapai County and beyond had come to help the newlyweds celebrate. Now that the pastor had introduced the old foreman and the pretty artist as man and wife, the reception was in full swing. Champagne corks were popping in all directions and live music floated across the rapidly cooling air.

Joseph and Tessa had gone all out to help give their devoted foreman a wedding to remember. The backyard had been set up with rows of tables decorated with flowers and loaded with food and drinks of all kinds. Paper lanterns had been strung from tree limbs and crisscrossed the wide parquet dance floor. Folding chairs, along with bales of hay, were grouped strategically away from the dancing area for those guests who chose to sit rather than stretch their legs to the music.

"This isn't the sort of music I would've expected to hear at a ranch wedding," Taggart said, as he twirled Emily-Ann across the makeshift dance floor.

"Sam and Gabby wanted to dance to standards, so Isabelle searched until she found a band from Phoenix who could play them well. Personally, I love it," she said, her eyes twinkling up at him. "It's very romantic. Especially when I'm dancing with my handsome husband."

Smiling he rubbed his nose against her forehead.

"My beautiful wife will always be a romantic. I just feel bad that you didn't have this big of a wedding."

She laughed. "Are you kidding? I didn't want the whole county at our wedding! Besides, we were in a hurry and Maureen and Camille and Isabelle rushed like crazy to get our ceremony pulled off. It was beautiful and I have a stack of photos to prove it."

"I don't need a photo to remember how you looked that day," he whispered near her ear. "You were a heavenly dream in your long ivory dress and tiny flowers pinned in your hair. Come to think of it, you look mighty heavenly right now."

"It's the extra hormones from being pregnant. Camille says it makes us glow," she said with an impish grin, then added with a wistful sigh, "I wish she and Matthew could've been here tonight. They were planning to come, you know. But her doctor advised against it. The baby could come at any time."

"I'm sure they're thinking about everyone." The song came to an end and Taggart led Emily-Ann off the platform. "Let's go have some punch. We'll dance again in a few minutes. I don't want to wear you out."

"Something to drink sounds good," she agreed.

The two of them made their way to one of the quieter tables set up near a pair of Joshua trees. Once there, Taggart filled two glass cups with punch and handed one of them to Emily-Ann.

As he sipped the fruity drink, his gaze drifted over the heads of the guests to where Gabby and

Sam were being monopolized by well-wishers. "The music isn't the only thing that's surprised me this evening," he said. "I wasn't expecting to see Sam in a Western-cut suit. He looks downright dignified."

Emily-Ann nodded. "Very handsome for a man of his age," she agreed. "And the way he looks at Gabby—it's obvious he adores her. And she gazes at Sam—well, like he hung the moon just for her. It's an inspiration seeing them together."

He cast a wry glance at his wife. "Well, there's another couple here tonight that looks to me like they're very much in love."

Moving closer, she slipped an arm around the back of his waist. "You mean us?"

Taggart tightened his hold on her waist while thinking it was indecent to feel this happy. Being married to Emily-Ann and sharing their home together on Three Rivers Ranch was like finding heaven on earth. Now that they had a child on the way, he was eagerly looking forward to being the father he'd always wanted and needed, but never had.

So far, Buck O'Brien hadn't tried to contact him, but the old man continued to make life hard for Tallulah. Taggart and Emily-Ann were both trying to persuade his sister to move here to Arizona. The last time he'd talked to her, he'd gotten the impression she was close to giving in.

"Other than us," he said, then inclined his head

toward the far end of the dance floor where Gil was guiding Maureen into a slow two-step.

Emily-Ann's gaze followed Taggart's. "Oh, you're talking about Maureen and Gil. Yes, the more I see them together, the more I'm sure she's completely gone on the man. Which I think is okay with all her children, don't you? I know for sure that Camille doesn't object. But guys are kind of different when it comes to their mothers—they can be possessive."

"You mean since Joel is gone, the guys might need to protect their mother from assertive males?"

"That's close to what I'm trying to say. Not that I think Gil is assertive. Quite the opposite. He's very nice. He even stops by the coffee shop when he's in town and always leaves me a tip."

Since they'd married, Emily-Ann was still working at Conchita's and planned to keep her job until the baby arrived. After that, she was going to take time off to be a mother and finish her nursing degree. At least, that's what she had planned. Taggart couldn't imagine her giving up the coffee shop job completely. Not when she loved it so much. But that was her choice. All he wanted was for her to be happy and to know that he loved her and the baby utterly.

"Gil is a stand-up guy," Taggart said. "I just wish—"

"What?" she prompted.

"Oh, that the mystery around Joel's death could

be solved," he said. "I think it would help Maureen put losing him behind her once and for all."

Her eyes full of love and tenderness, she reached up and touched a finger to his cheek. "And what about you, Tag? Have you put your losses behind you?"

The smile he gave her couldn't have been more honest. "All I see, my darling wife, is the future. With you and me and our children."

He had just finished placing a soft kiss on her lips when Chandler strode quickly over to them and from the look on his face, he had good news.

"We just heard from Matthew. Camille has delivered her baby. A boy—Matthew Harrison Waggoner."

"Sounds like he's going to be a junior," Emily-Ann stated.

Chandler shook his head as he jerked out his smartphone and held it out for them to see the tiny baby swaddled in a blue receiving blanket. "Matthew is calling him Harry for Harrison and since that was our maternal great grandfather's name, Camille is happy with it."

"Are she and the baby okay?" Taggart asked.

"Matthew snapped this pic before they carried the baby off to the nursery. He says everyone is great and little Harry has red hair like his mother."

"Oh my!" Emily-Ann exclaimed, then sniffed as joyous tears filled her eyes.

Spotting them, Taggart asked, "Honey, why are you crying at this wonderful news?"

She dabbed a finger beneath both eyes. "Camille wanted our babies to both be gingers—like the two of us. Now if mine doesn't turn out having red hair, she'll be terribly disappointed."

Both men laughed loudly and then Taggart wrapped a reassuring arm around her shoulders and squeezed her close to his side.

"Don't worry, sweetheart, if this baby of ours doesn't turn out to be a ginger, the next one will be."

Chandler winked at Taggart and gave him a playful swat on the arm. "Welcome to the family, Tag."

* * * * *

Don't miss the next Men of the West story, available in August 2020!

And for more great second chance at love romances, try these stories from Harlequin Special Edition:

Her Homecoming Wish *by Jo McNally*
A Baby Affair *by Tara Taylor Quinn*
Second-Chance Sweet Shop *by Rochelle Alers*

Available now!

#2761 BETTING ON A FORTUNE
The Fortunes of Texas: Rambling Rose • by Nancy Robards Thompson
Ashley Fortune is furious Rodrigo Mendoza has been hired to consult on her new restaurant and vows to send him packing. Soon her resentment turns to attraction, but Rodrigo won't mix business with pleasure. When her sister gives her a self-help book that promises to win him over in a week, Ashley goes all in to land Rodrigo's heart!

#2762 THEIR SECRET SUMMER FAMILY
The Bravos of Valentine Bay • by Christine Rimmer
Officer Dante Santangelo doesn't "do" relationships, but the busy single dad happily agrees to a secret summer fling with younger, free-spirited Gracie Bravo. It's the perfect arrangement. Until Gracie falls for Dante, his adorable twins and their ever-present fur baby!

#2763 HER SECOND FOREVER
The Brands of Montana • by Joanna Sims
The car accident that left her permanently injured made Lee Macbeth only more determined to help others with disabilities. Now there's a charming cowboy doing a stint of community service at her therapeutic riding facility and he wants more from the self-sufficient widow. Despite their powerful mutual attraction, Lee won't risk falling for Mr. Totally Wrong...will she?

#2764 STARTING OVER IN WICKHAM FALLS
Wickham Falls Weddings • by Rochelle Alers
Georgina Powell is finally moving out of her parents' house after years of carrying her mother's grief. At thirty-two years old, she's ready for a fresh start. She just didn't expect it to come in the form of Langston Cooper, the famed war correspondent who recently returned to buy Wickham Falls's local paper. But as she opens her own business, his role as editor in chief may steer him in a different direction—away from their future together.

#2765 THE RELUCTANT FIANCÉE
The Taylor Triplets • by Lynne Marshall
When Brynne Taylor breaks off her engagement to Paul Capriati, she knows her life is going to change. But when two women who claim to be triplets to her show up in her small Utah town, it's a lot more change than she ever expected. Now she's digging up long-buried family secrets and navigating her relationship with her ex-fiancé. Does she actually want to get married?

#2766 THE NANNY'S FAMILY WISH
The Culhanes of Cedar River • by Helen Lacey
Annie Jamison has dreamed of capturing the heart of David Culhane McCall. But she knows the workaholic widower sees her only as a caregiver to his children. Until her resignation lands on his desk and forces him to acknowledge that she's more than just the nanny to him. Is he ready to risk his heart and build a new family?

HSECNM0420

*Officer Dante Santangelo doesn't "do" relationships,
but the busy single dad happily agrees to a secret
summer fling with younger free-spirited Gracie Bravo.
It's the perfect arrangement. Until Gracie realizes
she wants a life with Dante. Either she can say goodbye
at the end of the summer...or risk everything to
make this family happen.*

Read on for a sneak preview of
New York Times *bestselling author Christine Rimmer's
next book in the Bravos of Valentine Bay miniseries,*
Their Secret Summer Family.

"Gracie, will you look at me?"

Stifling a sigh, she turned her head to face him. Those melty brown eyes were full of self-recrimination and regret.

"I'm sorry," he said. "I never should have touched you. I'm too old for you, and I'm not any kind of relationship material, anyway. I don't know what got into me, but I swear to you it's never going to happen again."

Hmm. How to respond?

Too bad there wasn't a large blunt object nearby. The guy deserved a hard bop on the head. What was wrong with him? No wonder it hadn't worked out with Marjorie. The man didn't have a clue.

But never mind. Gracie held it together as he apologized some more. She watched that beautiful mouth move and pondered the mystery of how such a great guy could have his head so far up his own ass.

Maybe if she yanked him close and kissed him, he'd get over himself and admit that last night had been amazing, the two of them had off-the-charts chemistry and he didn't want to walk away from all that goodness, after all.

Yeah, kissing him might shut him up and get him back on track for more hot sexy times. It had worked more than once already.

But come on. She couldn't go jumping on him and smashing her mouth on his every time he started beating himself up for having a good time with her.

No. A girl had to have a little pride.

He thought last night was a mistake?

Fair enough. She'd actually let herself believe for a minute or two there that they had something good going on, that her long dry spell manwise might be over.

But never mind about that. Let him have it his way. She would agree with him.

And then she would show him exactly what he was missing. And then, when he couldn't take it anymore and begged her for another chance, she would say that they couldn't, that he was too old for her and it wouldn't be right.

Don't miss
Their Secret Summer Family *by Christine Rimmer,*
available May 2020 wherever
Harlequin Special Edition books and ebooks are sold.

Harlequin.com

HSEEXP0420

Powerfully emotional, *New York Times* bestselling author

MAISEY YATES'S

new novel is a heartwarming exploration of how life's biggest challenges can turn into the greatest opportunities of all...

Secrets from a Happy Marriage

Order your copy today!

HQN

HQNBooks.com

PHMYBPA0520

Love Harlequin romance?

DISCOVER.

Be the first to find out about promotions, news and exclusive content!

Facebook.com/HarlequinBooks

Twitter.com/HarlequinBooks

Instagram.com/HarlequinBooks

Pinterest.com/HarlequinBooks

ReaderService.com

EXPLORE.

Sign up for the Harlequin e-newsletter and download a free book from any series at **TryHarlequin.com**

CONNECT.

Join our Harlequin community to share your thoughts and connect with other romance readers!
Facebook.com/groups/HarlequinConnection